BACK OF BEYOND

BEYOND

STORIES OF THE SUPERNATURAL

OTHER BOOKS BY SARAH ELLIS

A Family Project

Next-Door Neighbors

Pick-Up Sticks

Out of the Blue

(Margaret K. McElderry Books)

SARAH ELLIS

BACK OF BEYOND

STORIES OF THE SUPERNATURAL

Margaret K. McElderry Books

For Barbara, Betty, Cathie, Greg, Joan, Maggie,
Martha, Nancy, Susan, and in memory of Paul and Ethel:
Friends across the line.

Margaret K. McElderry Books
An imprint of Simon & Schuster Children's Publishing Division
1230 Avenue of the Americas
New York, New York 10020

Designed by Nina Barnett
The text of this book is set in Perpetua.

Printed in the United States of America
10 9 8 7 6 5 4 3
Library of Congress Cataloging-in-Publication Data
Ellis, Sarah.
Back of beyond : stories of the supernatural / by Sarah Ellis.—
1st U.S. ed.
p. cm.
Summary: A collection of twelve otherworldly stories which blend
reality and unreality.
ISBN 0-689-81484-4
1. Reality—Juvenile fiction. 2. Children's stories, American.
[1. Reality—Fiction. 2. Short stories.] I. Title.
PZ7.E4758Baj   1997
[Fic]—dc21
97-6844 CIP AC

12.75

Most "fairy" experiences are unspectacular, private affairs, unaccountable little slippages in space or time, oddities pondered from time to time by the people involved, maybe shared if someone asks. Small people dance in a Patrick Street garden, an invisible wall rises in a marsh, a scrubby patch of trees becomes a boundless wilderness: little fairy tricks, and suddenly everyday reality is open to question.

—Barbara Rieti, *Strange Terrain:*
The Fairy World in Newfoundland

CONTENTS

TUNNEL

When I was a kid and I imagined myself older and with a summer job, I thought about being outdoors. Tree planting, maybe. Camping out, getting away from the parents, coming home after two months with biceps of iron and bags of money. I used to imagine myself rappelling down some mountain with a geological hammer tucked into my belt. At the very worst I saw myself sitting on one of those tall lifeguard chairs with zinc ointment on my lips.

I didn't know that by the time I was sixteen it would be the global economy and there would be no summer jobs, even though you did your life-skills analysis as recommended by the guidance counselor at school. Motivated! Energetic! Computer literate! Shows initiative! Workplace-appropriate hair! What I never imagined was that by the time I got to be sixteen the only job you could get would be baby-sitting.

I sometimes take care of my cousin Laurence. Laurence likes impersonating trucks and being held upside down. I am good at assisting during these activities. This evidently counts as work-related experience.

Girls are different.

Elizabeth, who calls herself Ib, is six and one-quarter years old. I go over to her place at 7:30 in the morning and I finish at one o'clock. Then her dad or her mom or her gran (who is not really her gran but the mother of her dad's ex-wife) takes over. Ib has a complicated family. She doesn't seem to mind.

Ib has a yellow plastic suitcase. In the suitcase are Barbies. Ib would like to play with Barbies for five and one-half hours every day. In my baby-sitting course at the community center they taught us about first aid, diapering, nutritious snacks, and how to skip to my Lou. They did not teach Barbies.

"You be Wanda," says Ib, handing me a nude Barbie who looks as though she is having a bad hair life.

I'm quite prepared to be Wanda if that's what the job requires. But once I *am* Wanda I don't know what the heck to do.

Ib is busy dressing Francine, Laurice, Betty, and Talking Doll, who is not a Barbie at all, but a baby doll twice the size of the Barbies.

"What should I do?" I ask.

Ib gives me the Look, an unblinking stare that combines impatience, scorn, and pity.

"Play," she says.

When you have sixteen-year-old guy hands, there is no way to hold a nude Barbie without violating her personal space. But all her clothes seem to be made of extremely form-fitting stretchy neon stuff, and I can't get her rigid arms with their poky fingers into the sleeves.

Playing with Barbies makes all other activities look good. The study of French irregular verbs, for example, starts to seem attractive. The board game Candyland, a favorite of Cousin Laurence, and previously condemned by me as a sure method for turning the human brain to tofu, starts to seem like a laff riot.

I look at my watch. It is 8:15. The morning stretches ahead of me. Six weeks stretch ahead of me. My life stretches ahead of me. My brain is edging dangerously close to the idea of eternity.

I hold Wanda by her hard, clawlike plastic hand and think of things that Laurence likes to do. We could notch the edge of yogurt lids to make deadly star-shaped weapons for a Ninja attack, but somehow I don't think that's going to cut it with Ib. She's probably not going to go for a burping contest, either.

A warm breeze blows in the window, a small wind that probably originated at sea and blew across the beach, across all those glistening, slowly browning bodies, before it ended up here, trapped in Barbie World. I'm hallucinating the smell of suntan oil. I need to get outside.

I do not suggest a walk. I know, from Laurence, that "walk" is a four-letter word to six-year-olds. Six-year-olds can run around for seventy-two hours straight, but half a block of walking and they suffer from life-threatening exhaustion. I therefore avoid the *W* word.

"Ib, would you like to go on an exploration mission?"

Ib thinks for a moment. "Yes."

We pack up the Barbies.

"It's quite a long way," I say. "We can't take the suitcase."

"I need to take Wanda."

We take Wanda.

We walk along the overgrown railway tracks out to the edge of town. Ib steps on every tie. The sun is behind us and we stop every so often to make our shadows into letters of the alphabet.

("And what sort of work experience can you bring to this job, young man?"

"Well, sir, I spent one summer playing with Barbie dolls and practicing making my body into a *K*."

"Excellent! We've got exciting openings in that area.")

We follow the tracks as the sun rises high in the sky. Ib walks along the rail holding my hand. My feet crunch on the sharp gravel and Ib sings something about ducks. I inhale the dusty smell of sun-baked weeds and I'm pulled back to the summer that we used to come out here, Jeff and Danielle and I. That was the summer that Jeff was a double agent planning to blow up the enemy supply train.

The sharp sound of a pneumatic drill rips through the air and Ib's hand tightens in mine.

"What's that?"

I remember. "It's just a woodpecker."

There was a woodpecker once back then, too.

"Machine-gun attack!" yelled Jeff. And I forgot it was a game and threw myself down the bank into the bushes. Jeff laughed at me.

"No little ducks came swimming back." Ib's high, thin voice is burrowing itself into my brain and there is a pulse above my left eye. I begin to wish I had brought something to drink. Maybe it's time to go back.

And then we come to the stream. I hear it before I see it. And then I remember what happened there.

Ib jumps off the tracks and dances off toward the water.

I don't want to go there. "Not that way, Ib."

"Come *on,* Ken. I'm exploring. This is an exploration mission. You said."

I follow her. It's different. The trees—dusty, scruffy-looking cottonwoods—have grown up and the road appears too soon. But there it is. The stream takes a bend and disappears into a small culvert under the road. Vines grow across the entrance to the drainage pipe. I push them aside and look in. A black hole with a perfect circle of light at the end.

It's so small. Had we really walked through it? Jeff and Danielle and finally me, terrified, shamed into it by a girl and a double dare.

I take a deep breath and I'm there again. That smell. Wet and green and dangerous. There I was, feet braced against the pipe, halfway through the tunnel, at the darkest part. I had kept my mind up, up out of the water where Jeff said that blackwater bloodsuckers lived. I kept my mind up until it went into the weight of the earth above me. Tons of dirt and cars and trucks and being buried alive.

Dirt pressing heavy against my chest, against my eyelids, against my legs which wouldn't move. And then, above the roaring in my ears, I heard a high snatch of song, two notes with no words. Calling. I pushed against the concrete and screamed without a sound.

And then Jeff yelled into the tunnel, "What's the matter, Kenny? Is it the bloodsuckers? Kenton, Kenton, where are you? Ve vant to suck your blood." Jeff had a way of saying "Kenton" that made it sound like an even finkier name than it is. By this time I had peed my pants and I had to pretend to slip and fall into the water to cover up. The shock of the cold. The end of the tunnel. Jeff pushed me into the stream because I was wet anyway. Danielle stared at me and she knew.

*   *   *

"Where does it go?" Ib pulls on my shirt.

And I'm big again. Huge. Like Talking Doll.

"It goes under the road. I walked through it once."

"Did you go to that other place?"

"What other place?"

Ib gives me the Look. "Where those other girls play. I think this goes there."

Yeah, right. The Barbies visit the culvert.

Ib steps right into the tunnel. "Come on, Kenton."

I grab her. "Hey! Hold it. You can't go in there. You'll . . . you'll get your sandals wet. And I can't come. I don't fit."

Ib sits down on the gravel and takes off her sandals. "I fit."

Blackwater bloodsuckers. But why would I want to scare her? And, hey, it's just a tunnel. So I happen to suffer from claustrophobia. That's my problem.

"Okay, but look, I'll wait on this side until you're halfway through and then I'll cross over the road and meet you on the other side. Are you sure you're not scared?"

Ib steps into the pipe and stretches to become an *X*. "Look! Look how I fit!"

I watch the little *X* splash its way into the darkness. "Okay, Ib, see you on the other side. Last one there's a rotten egg." I let the curtain of vines fall across the opening.

I pick up the sandals and climb the hill. It's different, too. It used to be just feathery horsetail and now skinny trees grow there. I grab on to them to pull myself up. I cross the road, hovering on the center line as an RV rumbles by and then I slide down the other side, following a small avalanche of pebbles. I kneel on the top of the pipe and stick my head in, upside down.

"Hey, rotten egg, I beat you."

Small, echoing, dripping sounds are the only answer.

I peer into the darkness. She's teasing me.

"Ib!"

Ib, Ib, Ib—the tunnel throws my voice back at me. A semi-trailer roars by on the road. I jump down and stand at the pipe's entrance. My eyes adjust and I can see the dim green *O* at the other end. No outline of a little girl. A tight heaviness grips me around the chest.

"Ibbie. Answer me right now. I mean it." I drop the sandals.

She must have turned and hidden on the other side, just to fool me.

I don't remember getting up the hill and across the road, except that the noise of a car horn rips across the top of my brain.

She isn't there. Empty tunnel.

"Elizabeth!"

She slipped. She knocked her head. Child drowns in four inches of bathwater.

I have to go in. I try walking doubled over. But my feet just slip down the slimy curved concrete and I can only shuffle. I drop to my hands and knees.

Crawl, crawl, crawl, crawl.

The sound of splashing fills my head.

Come back, Elizabeth.

Do not push out against the concrete. Just go forward, splash, splash.

Do not think up or down.

Something floats against my hand. I gasp and jerk upward, cracking my head. It's Wanda. I push her into my shirt. My knee bashes into a rock and there is some sobbing in the echoing tunnel. It is my own voice.

And then I grab the rough ends of the pipe and pull myself into the light and the bigness.

Ib is crouched at the edge of the stream pushing a floating leaf with a stick. A green light makes its way through the trees above.

She looks up at me and sees Wanda poking out of my shirt. "Oh, good, you found her. Bad Wanda, running away."

My relief explodes into anger.

"Ib, where were you?"

"Playing with the girls."

"No, quit pretending. I'm not playing. Where were you when I called you from the end of the tunnel? Were you hiding? Didn't you hear me call?"

"Sure I heard you, silly. That's how they knew my name. And I was going to come back but it was my turn. They never let me play before, but this time they knew my name and I got to go into the circle. They were dancing. Like ballerinas. Except they had long hair. I get to have long hair when I'm in grade two."

My head is buzzing. I must have hit it harder than I realized. I hand Wanda to Ib and grab at some sense. "Why didn't you come when I called you?"

"They said I wasn't allowed to go, not while I was in the circle, and they were going to give me some cake. I saw it. It had sprinkles on it. And then you called me again but you said 'Elizabeth.' And then they made me go away."

Ib blows her leaf boat across the stream. And then she starts to sing.

"Idey, Idey, what's your name,
What's your name to get in the game."

That song, the two-note song. The sweet high voice calling to me in the tunnel. The sound just before Jeff yelled at me. The sound just before Jeff called me back by my real name.

The final puzzle piece of memory slides into place. They wanted me. They wanted Ib. I begin to shiver.

I find myself sitting on the gravel. The stream splashes its way over the lip of the pipe into the tunnel. I stare at Ib, who looks so small and so solid. My wet jeans with their slime-green knees begin to steam in the sun. A crow tells us a thing or two.

"Ken?"

"Yes?"

"I don't really like those girls."

"No, they don't sound that nice. Do you want to go home?"

"Okay."

I rinse off my hands and glance once more into the darkness.

"Put on your sandals, then."

Ib holds on to the back belt loops of my jeans and I pull her up the hill, into the sunshine.

POTATO

Dad met me at the front door. "Nathan is back."

The duffel bag slid out of my fingers and landed on my foot. "Where is he?"

"Up in his room."

I turned toward the stairs.

"Selina? He'll join us when he's ready. Give him time."

"Is he . . . okay?"

Dad took my hand and squeezed it. "I hope so."

I went upstairs. Nathan's door was shut. I stared at it. There wasn't a sound. I put my ear to the door. He couldn't be asleep because there wasn't any snoring.

Nathan is a grand master snorer. A couple of years ago, when Dad tore the back off the house, our bedrooms disappeared and Nathan and I had to camp out in the living room for a month. Every night it was the same. I would sink into sleep and then— RUMBLE, SNORT, GAG, WHISTLE, GURGLE. Pause. Repeat. For hours.

He wouldn't believe he did it. He said that I made it up. He said that I was systematically undermining his feelings of self-worth so that when the time came I would inherit the family business. The family business is Farkell's Janitorial Supplies. Like we're both dying to inherit it.

One night when he was at full-blast, window-rattling volume, I got up and turned the tape deck to record. The next morning when I presented him with the evidence, he accused me of doctoring the tape with technical assistance from the CIA. I threw a pillow at his adenoidal head.

If he wasn't asleep, what was he doing in there? There is absolutely nothing to do in Nathan's room. By the time he left, it was almost completely bare. Empty bookshelves, no rug or curtains or lampshades, rectangular shapes on the walls where the posters used to be. No radio. Dad called it the sensory deprivation tank.

Getting rid of his stuff was the first weird thing Nathan did when he started to change. At first Mom thought it was fine, that he was finally digging out his room. But I knew it was wrong. Nathan loved old stuff. He could smell a good junk store from ten blocks away. This was a guy who grew ecstatic over ugly menswear, plastic ukuleles, Hot Wheels, tube amplifiers, and Smurfiana.

I'm low on collector genes myself but one Saturday I did go with Nathan on a garage sale crawl. As we progressed from sale to sale, he tried unsuccessfully to interest me in salt-and-pepper shakers, children's books, baseball caps.

"This could be the start of a fabulous collection," he enthused.

After I had refused to part with my hard-earned baby-sitting money for a copy of *Tizard the Lizard Goes on a Spree,* he gave up in frustration and bought me a box of assorted pencils.

"You can't go home empty-handed."

By late afternoon we were on our fifth sale and Nathan's haul consisted of a flip-front toaster, a Country Joe and the Fish album, a neon Husky Tower tie, and a Smurf lunch box. I was starting to suffer from an overdose of stuff when Nathan suddenly went tense. He was staring at a pile of board games. His nostrils widened slightly.

"Is it . . . ?" He gently wiggled a small box from halfway down the pile. "It *is!* Mr. Potato Head!"

I looked in the box. It was a set of plastic facial features, with little pegs on the back of each piece. Eyes, eyebrows, a mouth.

"The real thing! Not those stupid modern ones that you stick on a plastic potato. Look at this, it even has the pipe. Smoking! How incorrect. This is seriously fabulous."

Nathan paid his fifty cents for Mr. Potato Head and we got in the car. Nathan pushed back in his seat and extended his arms stiffly toward the steering wheel. "That's so good. Follow your bliss to Mr. Potato Head." He pulled out into traffic. "Ah, the triumph of the hunt. Poised at the edge of the ice floe a young man waits. Alert, silent, motionless. Then, at some subtle signal, he is galvanized into action. The pounce, the kill, the prize."

I snorted. "And the trophy is a Smurf lunch box? Get a grip."

Nathan smiled his revolting big-brother smile. "Oh, you couldn't be expected to understand. It's a man against the elements. It's a guy thing."

I had to wait until a red light before I had a chance to beat him up.

When we got home, we found a couple of potatoes and brought Mr. Potato Head to life as Mr. Normal, Sam Spud the hard-boiled private investigator, Cyclops, and the Confused Smoker (pipe up the nose). But the best was my invention. I peeled one of the potatoes, leaving just a strip of peel across the top, Mohawk-style. Then I added a drawn-on skull tattoo and a pull-tab nose ring. He looked really bad.

"Potato with an attitude," said Nathan. "Mr. Baad-ato."

We put him on the toothbrush holder in the bathroom with a sign: GO AHEAD. MAKE MY DAY.

That all happened before, before Nathan stopped smiling and talking, before he started getting rid of things. One day on my way to school, I noticed a paper shopping bag next to the garbage can behind the garage. It contained all of Nathan's best things, his lava lamp, his vinyl 45s, and the Mr. Potato Head kit.

He wasn't just cleaning up his room. He was giving himself away, piece by piece. I took Mr. Potato Head back and kept him in my room.

But I couldn't hold on to Nathan. He slipped away. Especially after he went on the seabird rescue mission. Last year there was an oil spill off the coast. Nathan saw the oil-soaked birds on TV and the next day he left. He missed his final exams.

When he came home he was very quiet. When I told him my latest idea for our "Restaurants We Don't Want to Visit" contest, "Pizza 'n Parsnips," he didn't even smile. He didn't want to read the latest janitorial supplies catalog in his Bela Lugosi horror voice. He just kept looking at me as if I were a Martian.

One night I was walking by his bare room and he called me in. He was sitting cross-legged on his bed.

"What, are you in training to be a monk?" I asked.

He didn't answer or even smile. There was a kind of pleading look in his eyes.

"Selina, it's going rotten."

"What?"

"Just being here. Breathing, drinking water."

"You mean like pollution and the ozone and all that?"

"We're gobbling it all up and spewing out garbage. Sometimes I feel like we're vermin covering the earth." He closed his eyes in a long blink. "Those sea otters, covered in oil. They bleed from the nose before they die."

I reached over and touched the nearest part of him, his foot. "But that's not you. That's not your fault. You were even helping. Nathan, what is it?"

He just stared. I don't think he even heard me, or felt me. "I'm the poison."

It did get better for a while. Dad said if Nathan was going to flunk out of college, he had to work. So he got some sort of job doing a survey of people's opinions on the transit service. And he seemed to have some friends. Not his old friends like Allison and Francesca and Bernard, but people he talked to on the phone.

I saw him on the job once. Miriam and I were on our way downtown to a movie and we transferred buses and there he was, standing with a clipboard on the corner. There was another guy with a clipboard beside him. We went up and pretended we didn't know him and started to answer the survey. We said that we traveled on transit about eleven times daily and that we thought the service could be improved with onboard videos. Nathan didn't play. He was jumpy and he kept glancing nervously at the other clipboard guy beside him. Then that guy took over and asked us if we ever felt overwhelmed or lacking in confidence. This seemed a pretty strange question for a transit survey. Miriam started to invent an adolescent alcohol abuse problem and then we both got the giggles. Then Nathan smiled and my giggles dried up. His face wasn't right. It was like one of those computer faces, ASCII art. At a glance it looks like a person, but if you stare close up, it is just a bunch of little numbers and letters. I took Miriam away.

There was still no sound from Nathan's room. I slid down the wall and sat on the floor, resting my chin on my knees. I pulled bits of fuzz off the carpet. I faked a sneeze and waited. No response. I needed to talk to him, to unsay the last thing I said to him before he left.

The last morning—but I didn't know that—he seemed like his old self, humming with energy. He told me to come out onto the back porch and then he put his hand on my shoulder and pointed at the sky. It was one of those cottage-cheese-cloud days. "I'm going to tell you," he said. "I can't tell Mom and Dad because they are not ready to hear. But I think you are ready to hear."

Ready to hear?

"It is going to be fine. The master has the answer. We must just align ourselves for the special moment."

It was the "special moment" that did it. Nathan used to *hate* the word "special." He used to put on a sickie-sweet voice and say, "I'm special, you're special, we're all special, boys and girls," whenever he heard the word and then he'd stick his finger down his throat. Where was that Nathan? His hand on my shoulder felt heavy and hot. I threw it off.

"Stop talking like a weirdo. What's with you, anyway? You're turning into a freak."

And he just smiled at me. The ASCII smile.

When I came home from school that day he was gone. He left a note for Mom and Dad. It was more gobbledygook about harmony and a sanctuary for the chosen. The police couldn't do anything because Nathan is an adult and free to leave home. Allison said that Nathan had talked about some group called the Harmonic Order of the Universal Mind. Bernard searched all over the Internet trying to find out something about them, but he came up with nothing.

It was like Nathan had been sucked into a void. But he didn't quite disappear. Every so often he phoned home. Mom always asked him if he was eating properly. Dad asked if he needed money.

We got call display on our phone so that we could trace the calls. They were all coming from the Seattle area but from phone booths. One day when I came home, Bernard and Dad were sitting at the kitchen table putting Post-it dots on a map of Seattle.

"They are all in roughly the same area," said Bernard.

Dad nodded. "What about this weekend?"

I pulled up a chair. "What's up?"

"Bernard and I are going to Seattle to look for Nathan," said Dad, poring over the map and not looking up at me.

"I want to come."

"Oh, Selina, that wouldn't be a good idea. We'll be in some rough areas late at night."

"I could help."

Dad's eyes were back on the map. "Not this time, sweetheart."

He sounded as though he was telling me I couldn't have an ice-cream cone. He sounded as though he had already forgotten I was there. Nathan was the one who was gone, but he was treating me like I was the one who had disappeared. I lost it.

"So who did he talk to before he left? You? Who did he say was ready to hear? You? So you find him, what makes you think he'll talk to you? Or come home?"

Dad looked like someone who has been jolted awake. He didn't say anything.

"I think she's right," said Bernard. "It would be useful if she came."

"But she's only fourteen," said Dad.

Bernard spoke softly. "Lots of kids on the street are fourteen."

Dad laid both hands, palm down, on the map. "Okay."

We got to Seattle in time for supper. It was a warm soft evening, a good evening for a picnic or a baseball game. Our hotel was only about a fifteen-minute walk from the area that Nathan's calls had come from. But in that fifteen minutes we entered another world, a gray world of warehouses and bars and boarded-up buildings.

We started out all together but it didn't work. Nobody would talk to us. "We look too much like a posse," said Bernard. "We'll have to split up. I'll take Selina." Dad wasn't happy but he gave us a wad of dollar bills and some copies of a photo of Nathan. We arranged to meet every hour.

The first lead, which turned out to be the only lead, happened right away. Bernard had dropped into a convenience store to get a cup of coffee and I was standing outside at the bus stop. Two young women came up to me. They were carrying clipboards.

"Would you be willing to answer a few questions about transit service?" one said. "It won't take more than five minutes of your time."

I remembered Nathan's so-called job and the weirdo guy he had been with. This was it, the same group.

I should have played along, at least until Bernard came back. But I blew it. I started asking questions. "Who's running this survey? Who are you anyway? What's your group?" I wanted to show them Nathan's picture but the photos were with Bernard. And then they just melted away. How could I follow them? I couldn't just leave. I tried to peer into the store but the windows were painted over. By the time Bernard came out I was crying with frustration.

We started to walk around the streets. At first I didn't see anyone we could talk to. But then I started to notice them, people in doorways and on benches, the people who lived there. It was like one of those puzzle drawings where you search for the bunny in the tree trunk and the frog in the clouds.

We talked to people who had long stories and people who were silent, to people who seemed so old that I didn't think they could still be alive and to kids my own age, younger maybe. We talked to people surrounded by bags and shopping carts of stuff and to people who had one Styrofoam cup. Some people swore at us, one woman spat on my shoe, and a twitchy skinny young man said, "God bless you."

Once we started to go along a path across a scrubby park and Bernard, who was just ahead of me, wheeled around abruptly and turned me around by my shoulders and marched me back.

"We don't want to go there," he said. I didn't ask why. I discovered that I didn't want to look too closely, I didn't want to know everything.

We showed Nathan's picture and we gave out dollar bills. We went into a storefront mission where a beautiful woman with red hair was cutting an old man's toenails. She took Nathan's picture and wished us luck.

I stared at the phone booth where Nathan had made some of his calls. I went in. It smelled like pee.

We met Dad every hour. At eleven o'clock he said, "Well, I met someone who knew him."

"Who?" I asked. "Does he know where he is now?"

Dad gave a sad smile. "Old guy. Vet. One leg. Told me he remembered Nathan from the Burma campaign. Asked me to give him his love. I said I would."

Around midnight it began to drizzle and the people disappeared. We gave up. As we headed back toward the hotel, we saw one last bundle of rags in a doorway. There was no face visible, just a hand. Dad didn't try to show Nathan's picture or ask a question. He just put the rest of the money into the hand. It disappeared into the clothes like a lizard into a stone wall.

My feet were wet and I felt bruised, bruised from the inside out. We didn't say much as we walked back. When we got to the hill leading up to the hotel, Dad took my hand. He held it hard. We both pretended that he was just helping me up the slope.

The next day we went home. Nathan never phoned again.

He had disappeared completely and now he was back. I stared at the door and thought of how I had everything and nothing to say to him.

I stood up and went to my room. Sitting on my desk were two eyes, two eyebrows, a nose, a mouth, two ears, a cap, a mustache, and a pipe: Mr. Potato Head. The features were arranged like a flattened face. I had done it last night.

Last night Mom and Dad were yelling. It was late, close to midnight. They woke me up. And I so much wanted to go into Nathan's room and for it to be full of stuff and for him to be there and for us to turn on some music with the bass cranked up to max. So I got out of bed and turned on my own music, loud. I went to my desk and took the Mr. Potato Head box out of the drawer. I cleared a space on the top of the desk and laid out the pieces. Surprise, anger, fear—the many faces of Mr. P. H. Then I turned the mouth a bit sideways and he looked like somebody who says funny things. The face blurred and I whispered to him, "Nathan, please come home."

I know, I know. Talking to little pieces of plastic.

I rearranged the potato eyebrows. When was Nathan going to come out of his room? Give him time. Wasn't nearly five months enough time? I got up and listened at his door again. Still nothing. I went down to the kitchen and looked in the vegetable bin. How could there be no potatoes? There are always potatoes. I opened the fridge, pulled out a stick of celery, and took it upstairs.

It is hard to fit all the Potato Head features onto a stick of celery. I had to omit the pipe. I made a sign: MR. CELERY HEAD WELCOMES YOU HOME. I put it all outside Nathan's door, knocked once, and ran back to my own room. I sat down at my desk.

Nathan didn't knock. He came right in. He knelt on the floor and hugged me. I felt all his ribs. I stayed in the bony hug because I was afraid to look in his eyes.

"I thought I put Mr. Potato Head in the garbage."

"I rescued him."

"You rescued him and he rescued me."

What? Was he going to start talking crazy again? I pulled away.

Nathan knew why. "No, it's okay. It's strange but it's okay. But I have to tell you this. Come down here."

We both sat down on the floor and Nathan propped Mr. Celery Head against my dresser. I looked at my brother. His head was shaved. He had a sore on his lip. But his real eyes were there.

Darker than I remember, but there.

"Last night I was on the street selling flowers . . ."

"Flowers?"

"We sell flowers to raise money for the master."

I wasn't going to pretend to understand any more. I wasn't going to be careful. "Who's the master?"

Nathan ran his hands over his face like a swimmer rubbing water out of his eyes. "I can't talk about that now. I'll tell you later."

"Okay."

"Last night I was selling in a great spot, outside a movie theater. When everyone came out from the late movie, they all wanted to buy flowers and I sold out in about twenty minutes. I sold the last bunch to a man who had a Mohawk and a nose ring and then I did a forbidden thing. I remembered Mr. Potato Head."

"Forbidden? What are you talking about?"

"We are forbidden to think about the life-before. But I did think of it and I remembered how good Mr. Baad-ato looked when he went moldy. And then I heard a clear voice saying, 'Come home.' And I panicked. I felt like there was all this space around me, a black hole, and that I was going to tumble into it."

Nathan spread his hands out on his knees. His fingernails were bitten down to the pink part. I had to look away.

"And then I did the second forbidden thing. I took the flower money and I did not return to the master. I walked to keep from falling. I came to a park. There was a van there, with a lineup of people. A man and a woman were giving away cups of coffee. I took one. Coffee is not permitted for the people. I made the man take all the money, the money for the master. And I drank the coffee."

Nathan's voice suddenly became like a chant. "No drugs, no

alcohol, no meat, no sex, no stimulants. The people. The chosen."
And he gave himself this punch in the chest.

I wanted to run away. It was too creepy. "What did you do next?"

Nathan swallowed. His Adam's apple stuck out. "I went over to a bench. The coffee woman brought me a blanket. I think I went to sleep. When the sun came up, the coffee van was gone. The money was in my pocket. And I saw that I was right across from the bus depot. There was a bus coming home."

Nathan picked up Mr. Celery Head. He looked at me with his real eyes and his eyebrows lifted just a bit. "Who would have thought that Mr. Potato Head would call me home?"

The real Nathan was back and I was suddenly filled with rage. It wasn't Mr. Potato Head, you jerk, it was *me,* your sister. But I didn't say that.

"How come you never once asked to speak to me when you phoned? How come you never asked about me?"

"It was forbidden."

"Oh, shut up about forbidden. Do you know what happened every single time you phoned? After, Mom would throw up and then later they would fight. Do you know what it's been like around here for five months? Do you care? Or is that 'forbidden,' too? And why did you go away, anyway?"

"Selina."

I looked at him through angry tears.

"I can't remember. I don't know because I can't remember. It is the life-before."

Nathan's eyes had the look of someone who is totally lost and frightened. My anger vaporized. All that time I just wanted Nathan to come home, the old Nathan, the goofball Nathan. But that person was gone. And the new Nathan, the weird one, the chosen one, he was gone, too, breaking up as I watched. What had happened to Nathan had changed him. He wouldn't ever leap back over it all.

And I thought of the night in Seattle, of all the people I had seen thrown away like garbage. I wasn't going to leap back either, to a Selina who didn't know about that world.

I reached over and grabbed Nathan's nail-bitten hand, the hand that was clenched around the celery. Mr. Potato Head, Mr. Celery Head, Mr. Parsnip Head, whatever. He was still my brother. Sometime soon I would tell him that.

PINCH

"Maps?"

"Check."

"Cooler?"

"Check."

"Tent?"

"Check."

"Whoopee cushion? Rubber chicken? False nose and mustache?"

"Check, check, check."

"We're all set then. Let's blow this Popsicle stand." Mom opened the front door.

"Ma-ni-to-ba here we come."

The phone rang.

I didn't like the sound of the ring. "Don't get it," I said.

"I'll just take it," she said, and lunged. "Yes? Yes, that's right but I'm just off . . . How far along? Oh, my goodness. Who's your family doctor?"

I closed the door.

"No prenatal care? No, no, don't panic . . ."

I sat down on the cooler.

"Yes, of course I'll come . . ."

I knew it.

She hung up. "That was the husband. His wife is in labor, fairly advanced it sounds like."

"Is this one of your patients at the clinic?"

"No, goodness knows how they got my number. But the poor guy. He's in quite a state."

I sighed. Not deliberately.

Mom gave me a hug. "Oh, I know. Look, I'll just go and send them off to emergency. They sound like they can't cope. We'll still get away tonight. They're sending a cab. Do you want to come along? Or you could invite Andrea over or something?"

The thought of staying in a house that I had already said good-bye to was pretty bleak.

"I'll come."

"Oh, good. Thanks, Maia. I'll just go change. A midwife in cut-offs might not inspire confidence."

I sat down in our very neat living room and felt squeezed. Mom could only take two weeks' vacation. It was going to take us three and a half days to drive to the lake, and the same back. That left seven days. Seven squeezed days. Now maybe six and a half. And this year Uncle Julius had a powerboat. There was going to be waterskiing. Travis and Melissa and the twins were going to be there for a whole month. They would have time to forget about time. Not me.

I traced the shape of an egg timer on the coffee table. Before, before Dad got sick, things were just bigger. Bigger rooms, a bigger yard, half-moons of orange peels marching across the kitchen counter from the juice he made every morning. And summers at the lake that went on forever.

Sometimes if I can't sleep I invent the future. It is full of *and*s. A girl *and* a boy *and* a girl. A big licky dog *and* a small bouncing dog *and* two cats *and* tropical fish for the one who has allergies. Evenings *and* weekends *and* holidays.

But for now the little grains of white sand fall in a thin line through that skinny little waist. We shop at Penny-Pinchers. We have a lot of *or*s. A movie *or* pizza. A skating pass *or* singing lessons. Paint for my room *or* repairs to the washing machine. Mom works six days a week and tries to find the time for everything else.

"Taxi's here." Mom grabbed her nurse bag. "You'd better bring a book."

The taxi took us to a part of the city where I had never been before. Interlocking crescents with big houses. The houses were mostly hidden behind hedges and fences. No corner stores or playgrounds or cars parked on the street. Lots of home security signs planted in front gardens.

We pulled into a wide, curving, steep driveway and I saw it first. A monkey puzzle tree.

I pinched Mom. "Monkey tree, no pinches back."

"Ouch!"

"It's your own fault. You taught me."

"Ah, yes, wanting to pass on my childhood traditions. Big mistake."

The house looked as big as a school. Pillars, wings, half-circle windows. The front door opened and a man in a suit came out. He paid the taxi driver and showed us inside. Mom explained about me and The Suit said, "Would you care to wait here for a moment, please." And he took Mom up some wide stairs.

I sat down and looked around. The front hall was as big as a tennis court. The floor was a checkerboard of black-and-white marble. Spaced around were short columns, like an ancient Greek ruin. The column next to my seat had a hologram set into it. I stared. It was a baton twirler in little white boots. I looked around at the back of her. The boots had tassels.

The walls were painted in a diamond pattern, dark red and gold. It was like a combination of King Arthur's court and the Pizza Palazzo designed by a very cheerful interior designer.

Around the doors some of the diamonds seemed to be raised. I wondered how snoopy I could be. There wasn't a sound. I sauntered over to the nearest door. The raised diamonds were movable. They swung aside to show light switches and outlets. I found myself smiling.

The Suit returned and apologized for keeping me waiting and thanked me so much for coming and wondered if I would like to wait in the media center. I got confused by this much politeness all at one time so I just said, "Sure."

By the time I had had the tour of the media center I was dizzy. Most of the time I didn't know what the heck The Suit was talking about. Laser this and digital that. All I managed to keep in my head was that there was a VCR with movies and a fridge with Coke. He left me with a remote that looked like the control panel of a spacecraft and the line, "If you need anything just ring."

Butler exits. Fade. Cut to commercial. Was this a movie or what?

I wandered around the room. Curved walls were lined with cupboards and sliding doors, screens, and machines, and heavy curtains closed over the windows. All the furniture was in the center of the room. There was a black wrought-iron chair shaped like a giant hand. On it was a large cushion, purple velvet, shaped like a glove. Hey! The velvet glove in the iron hand. Near it was a foot-stool shaped like a foot. I decided I liked this place.

I goofed around with the TV for a while wondering when Mom was going to get the woman to emergency. I found a menu of movies. I scrolled up and down. Every single movie I'd ever heard of was there. I helped myself to a Coke and some Cheezies. To think, I might have been home with basic cable. Then I happened upon some indexes. Director, studio, setting, type (screwball comedy, mindless violence, weepers), actor. For Andrea's sake I checked under Keanu Reeves. Andrea believes that she has a spiritual connection with Keanu Reeves. She has seen all his movies, even the ones where he only has about five words to say, even that one where he plays a stoned murderer with bad hair. She lights a candle in her room on his birthday. She's saving money to go on a pilgrimage to visit his elementary school in Toronto.

I read through the familiar titles and then, right at the bottom was something called *Words in the Deep*. I hadn't heard of that one. I pushed the load button. There he was, right in the opening scene, under the title. He's this sort of janitor working at some marine research place where scientists are trying to figure out how to communicate with dolphins. And it is all very secret because dolphins are the only hope for stopping some big ecological disaster and if the bad guys find out . . . Well, I couldn't quite figure out what the bad guys would do. But all the brilliant scientists are working against the clock, trying to decode dolphin speech, and one day Keanu Reeves, who is sort of a klutz, falls in the pool by mistake. And as soon as he is underwater, he can understand the dolphins perfectly.

By this point I had figured out what "variable screen" meant on the remote and I had expanded the TV screen until it was as big as the wall. A nine-foot Keanu swam by underwater. In his bathing suit. I rewound. The Suit came in with a message from Mom. They would not be going to the hospital and she would be a few more hours at least and she was sorry. I wasn't that disappointed. I wondered whether I, too, was developing a spiritual bond with Keanu.

So, anyway, he gets kidnapped by the bad guys. Then there are a bunch of high-speed boat chases. The wind blows through Keanu's shoulder-length hair. Dolphins leap about. And then I must have dozed because next thing I know the credits are rolling. Keanu and the dolphins are swimming around smiling so everything must have worked out okay.

I stood up and stretched, went over to the window, pushed back the curtains, and felt like I was back in the movie. Blue dappled light filled the room, reflections from the brightly lit pool just outside the window. It was like a small lake, shaped like a puddle, and it seemed to be half indoors, half out. The land fell away steeply on either side of the water and down at the far end of the pool were underwater windows.

There was a seat in the window with cushions and I curled up on it, letting the curtains fall shut behind me. As they closed I suddenly became convinced that the room behind them had disappeared. I stared at the heavy pleats and told myself to get a grip. But I couldn't help it. I twitched the curtains open again, fast, as though I was trying to fool someone. Everything was still there, hand chair and all. Of course. I flopped back against the cushions and made myself look outside. I imagined swimming under that tropical blue water and looking through the windows out across the water to the lights of downtown.

"Maia."

I was woken up by Mom's voice. There was a quilt over me.

Where was I? I couldn't get my brain moving. My mouth tasted like Cheezies. There was a faint light in the sky.

"Come on, Maia. Let's go home."

"Are you finished?"

"Yes, all's well. A big healthy boy. Lots of hair. Everybody's fine."

There was a taxi waiting in the courtyard. We crawled in.

Mom did a couple of neck rolls. "Quite the place, eh? I feel like Mother Hannah."

"Who's Mother Hannah?"

"She's a midwife in one of those old stories. She's called out in the middle of the night by a rider on a horse. She's blindfolded and taken to a palace, which turns out to be the home of the fairies. And she has to help with a fairy birth. It's a good story, very mysterious. Oh, right, then she gets this ointment in her eyes and the palace turns into a hut and the new mother is dressed in rags and lying on a heap of leaves. Or maybe that ointment thing is another story. There's a whole bunch about midwives and fairies. Makes sense to me. Labor *is* sort of like being in another world, beyond ordinary life, out of time. Might as well call it fairyland."

Mom leaned back and closed her eyes. "How did you do? Were you bored?"

"No way. They have a movie theater in there. You just dial up videos. It was excellent. You'd have to be brain-dead to be bored there."

Mom smiled. "Sounds like a lucky baby."

"For sure. Behind the house they have a huge pool, like Hollywood or something."

"Hollywood?" Mom sat up. "That reminds me. The bedroom

had the most amazing stuff in it. Like there were these green velvet curtains. At first I didn't pay that much attention. We were all pretty busy. But later, well, I burst right out laughing. Remember that scene in *Gone with the Wind* where Scarlett makes a dress out of curtains?"

"Uh-huh."

"Well, these curtains had a dress pattern printed on them, with all the things like 'cut two' and 'selvage.' They were great."

I would tell her about the chair later, on the long drive.

"They were really a sweet couple. Gentle and sort of jokey. And such a pretty baby, pointy ears. One funny thing though."

"What?"

"Well, most home births have lots of people around. Sisters and parents and friends. But this young woman just had her husband there. And after the baby's born, there's usually lots of phoning. But they didn't phone anyone. It seemed kind of lonely. Oh, I'm probably making all this up."

She slid an envelope out of her purse. "They're also kind of old-fashioned. I said I would send a bill but instead he handed me this. Sort of feudal." She slid her finger under the flap.

"Holy doodle!" A stack of bills fell out onto her lap. It was a big stack. They were big bills. "What the . . . do you think it's a mistake?"

I reached over and picked up the envelope. "Look, it says your name right here and 'with grateful thanks.'"

"Grateful is one thing but . . ." Mom looked stunned. I tried to count the number of bills she was holding and do some arithmetic. She leaned over to the taxi driver. "Change of plans. We'd like a detour to that never-closed bakery on First."

The sun was just coming up when we got home with a bag full

of baked goods and a fist full of bucks. Mom sat down right away and counted the money. Then she just shook her head. "Would you make some coffee?"

By the time I got back with two mugs, she was on the phone. "Five o'clock tonight? That's fine. And our arrival time? It's a six-hour flight? Oh, no, of course, the time change. Three-hour flight, three-hour time difference. Arrive at eleven local time. That'll be fine. Thank you."

She took a long swallow of coffee. "Forget driving. We're flying. Julius can pick us up at the airport."

"Yes! So we get a whole extra week!"

"*I* get a whole extra week. You get how long you want. I've left your return open."

The summer suddenly got bigger, a variable screen. "Good thing you answered the phone last night."

Mom grinned. Then yawned. "I'm just going to lie down here for a minute and then I'll do a bit of repacking."

Five minutes later I pried the coffee cup from her hands. She was out.

I was as awake as anything, jumpy even. I phoned Andrea. I forgot it was so early. She thought I was nuts but I bribed her with chocolate croissants.

I left a note and got out my bike. When I got to Andrea's, she was waiting but she had sheet marks on her face. "You're a maniac," she said. "And how come you aren't gone?"

I told her the whole story as we rode along the bike path.

There was, of course, one element of my narrative that captured her interest above all others.

"He has *never* been in a movie about porpoises."

"Well, maybe it didn't play here."

"*Maia,* I would know. I know every movie he has ever been in. I know what *ads* he has been in, for Pete's sake. I even know what movie he's working on at this moment and it's nothing about porpoises."

"Dolphins."

"Dolphins, porpoises. It has nothing to do with any sea mammal. At all."

"Andrea, I saw it."

"You dreamt it."

You don't dream a whole movie, but I sensed a did-didn't–did-too argument right up ahead. "Yeah, maybe. Want a croissant?"

We stopped and sat on a bench. The benches on the bike path are given in memory of people who have died. They have little gold plaques. This one said, REMEMBERING 'EDDIE' MCPHAIL. I traced the "EDDIE" with my finger. Edward? Edwin? Eduardo? Dad's name was Ian, a name too short to shorten. I asked Mom if we could buy one of those benches in memory of Dad, but she found out that they cost more than a thousand dollars.

The shadow of the hill behind us fell just along the edge of the bench so I had warm legs and cool arms. The chocolate in the croissants was just perfectly half melted.

"So where was this weird house, anyway?" Andrea was licking the crumbs out of the croissant bag.

"Out near the university but more toward the water."

"Want to go there?"

"It's up that long hill."

"Come on, we are fueled by croissants."

I didn't have any trouble finding the area. But once we got there, the streets all looked alike. We went up and down and around. Only a few cars passed us and we didn't see anybody walking. The rich stay inside a lot.

My legs were starting to protest and I was about to give up when I caught a glimpse of a monkey puzzle tree. And the driveway was curved and steep. But I had remembered it paved, not dirt. As I stood looking, a truck came out of the driveway onto the road.

"Is this it?" said Andrea.

"I don't know. Let's go see."

We pushed our bikes up the dusty, rutted road. At the top was a huge deep hole surrounded by a chain-link fence and some trailers and shacks. There was a bald man sitting on a lawn chair near the fence.

"Guess this isn't it," said Andrea. "Let's go."

"Wait a minute. Come on." We pushed our bikes up to the fence and looked down.

Just a big hole with a bulldozer at the bottom and a road spiraling out of it.

"Most expensive residence ever to be built in this little burg." It was the bald man.

I looked over at him.

"Yup, and you know where they'll be dropping a bundle? On the subtrades. I've heard that they're bringing marble guys in from Italy and some beveled-skylight genius up from California. It's going to be quite the deal." He held out his hand. "Hi, I'm Merv Petty. Used to be in construction myself. Till I got my heart attack. Now I'm an observer, a sidewalk superintendent. Ha-ha."

I wandered over and shook his hand. "Hi, I'm Maia. This is my friend Andrea."

"Pleased to meet you. So they're going to have this two-story glass conservatory and a huge swimming pool, indoor and out-door, convertible-like."

The hair rose on my arms. "With underwater windows?"

Mr. Petty looked surprised. Then he laughed. "That's right. I guess you read that article, too. Quite the deal."

I hadn't read any articles. "What used to be here?"

"Well, now that's quite the mystery. This property has been empty for as long as I can remember and I go way back, let me tell you. Can't imagine leaving such an expensive property undevel-oped for so long. Peppermint?" He handed Andrea a white paper bag.

His watch beeped. "Uh-oh. Have to get back. If I'm not in at eleven, on the dot, my daughter gets all worried. Because of the old heart, you know. Nice to chat with you. No, keep the mints. Take care now." And he folded up his chair and set off down the steep drive, walking very carefully.

I leaned my bike against the fence and sat down on the scrubby, dusty grass. Deep in the hole, the bulldozer took bites out of the wet clay. I sucked my peppermint and tried to catch the sun moving across the links in the fence. Little white grains of sand falling through the egg timer, minute by minute by minute. Past, present, future. A house yet to be built.

But it *did* happen. It was real. Coke fizzing in the glass and the crunch of Cheezies.

Last night. Last. Past. Who were they?

I rested my head against the fence, pushing my nose through one of the holes and lacing my fingers around the wire. What if the egg timer exploded? The grains of sand would fly all around, like fireworks, past and future all mixed up. What was it Mom said? Out of time. Like the birth of a baby. Like those days and nights in the hospital when Dad was dying. Day and night and clocks and schedules didn't matter. Everything happened out of time, but it was real. The most real thing.

"Are you okay, Maia?"

"What?" I pulled my nose out of the fence. "Yeah, I'm okay. But . . . Andrea?"

"Uh-huh."

"Have you ever thought that there might not be any now."

"Any what now?"

"Any now, any present. Like, when is now?"

"Well, now is now."

"Yeah, but as soon as you said that, it was past. It was then."

"But it wasn't past when I said it. It's just because you weren't ready. Look, I'm going to say 'now' and when I say it, it will be now and I want you to pay attention."

"Okay."

"I'm going to give you three. One, two, three, NOW! There. That's now."

I really had tried to feel the nowness of it. But it didn't quite work. "That was close but it took time for your words to go through the air, hit my eardrum, and get to my brain. So really, by the time I heard 'now,' it was then already. It's like there's this thin line of *nows* streaming by and you can't catch them. It's kind of scary."

Andrea screwed up her face and held it that way for a few seconds. "Nope, I can't do it. I can't get worried about it. Are there any more croissants?"

I nodded. "At home, almond ones."

"With marzipan inside?"

"I think so."

"Come on then, let's go. The NOW of eating almond croissants awaits us."

I just love Andrea.

We paused at the top of the hill. Andrea made revving noises. "This is going to be great."

"You go first."

"Okay." She gave one giant push and was off, her hair streaming out behind her helmet.

I looked down the steep hill and imagined that around the corner, at the bottom of the hill, there was a ramp, pointing off to the western horizon. I would take off into the sky. It would take just a moment to adjust, to regain control, to figure out how to ride the smooth road of air. But then I would gear up, and up, and up. Each effortless pedal stroke would take me faster and faster. Until I was going the same speed as time, like the plane. And wherever I was going, I would arrive at the same time I left. So every moment would be now.

I released the brakes and very slowly began to gather speed. I sucked in air over my peppermint-cool teeth, and the wind blew warm on my face.

KNIFE

Nobody pays much attention to new people at our school. We have the highest turnover rate of any high school in the city. Families move here, live in an apartment for a while, then move out to the 'burbs so they can have a carport and a lawn and a golden retriever. The kids learn English and figure out locker culture and then they're ready to move on as well. We're a kind of boot camp for the guerrilla warfare that is real high school. Mrs. Fitzgerald, who teaches urban geography, calls us a high-density transitional area.

In our graduating class there are only three people who were here from grade eight on. Hester Tsao, Don Apple, and me. Mrs. Fitzgerald calls us the core community. I call us stuck.

So, anyway, it wasn't much of a deal when the principal interrupted history last week to introduce a new student. Ron something-or-other with a lot of syllables. Ron was big. Not tall so much as wide. A red baseball cap shaded his eyes. Mrs. Fitzgerald put him in the desk in front of me, recently vacated by Maddy Harris. Maddy with the clicking beads in her hair. The back of Ron's head was not going to be as interesting, especially when Mrs. Fitzgerald made him turn his baseball cap around. "I have no objection to hats," she said, "but I need to check your eyes for vital signs." Mrs. F. has used this joke before, but in this school she gets a fresh audience frequently. Hester and Don and I don't mind.

Ron sat down without a word. He shifted uncomfortably, like maybe the desk was too small for him. Then the weirdest thing happened. I felt this damp chill, like when someone comes in from the cold in winter. But we're talking a sunny afternoon in May here. I thought I also caught a faint whiff of sea salt.

Mrs. F. came down the aisle to bring Ron his textbook. She was wearing a sleeveless dress. I didn't see any goose bumps. Meanwhile I was beginning to shiver and I pulled my hands up into my jacket sleeves.

Maybe I was getting sick. Maybe I was getting the flu. I leaned my forehead on my hand. Fever? I stuck out my tongue and rolled my eyes down to see if it was coated. I couldn't see my tongue, but my eyes were definitely starting to hurt. And what was that tingling in my right elbow? Wasn't that one of the first symptoms of the flesh-eating disease?

That was it. I certainly couldn't go to my father's for dinner next week in that condition. Especially not with Stevie there. It would be completely irresponsible to expose a five-year-old boy to a rare, highly infectious virus.

To understand why I would rather have a flesh-eating disease than dinner with my father, you have to know that I haven't seen him in six years. He took off the summer I was eleven. For the longest time I was sure he was coming home again and that everything was going to be the same, that our family was just in some temporary alternate reality that we would flip out of any minute. When the truth finally bored itself into my mind, I made the decision to hate him.

I took good care of my hating. I watered it and weeded it and pruned it. I backed it up on disk. I carried it with me all the time. It was always there, handy, if I wanted to take it out.

And now he's back. Of all the transitions in our transitional area, this is the one I never expected. I thought he was in the Middle East for good, around the curve of the world, out of the picture, part of a new family and nothing to do with me.

Mom says I have to go to visit him, even just once.

"It's all water under the bridge, Curt. And he *has* been good about child support all these years, that's one thing. Who knows, maybe you'll get to know each other again."

Yeah. Right. How about not.

"Curtis?"

There was something anticipatory in Mrs. F.'s tone, a question in the air. I did a quick survey of the blackboard. William Lyon Mackenzie. The Family Compact. Not much help there.

And then the bell rang.

Mrs. F. grinned. I knew she would say it. "Saved by the bell once again, Curtis. Have a pleasant weekend, ladies and gentlemen. Buy low, sell high, and don't forget the quiz on Monday."

Then it happened. In the dull roar of Friday afternoon liberation, Ron turned around slowly. The desk shifted with him. And he looked at me. His eyes were dark brown like a beer bottle. Pale eyelashes. His eyes locked with mine and I couldn't look away. My breath stopped in my throat. It seemed like he was looking at me forever, but it couldn't have been because the desks were still closing, the chairs still scraping, far, far away. He put his hand on my desk. I tore my gaze away and looked down. His hand was closed into a fist. He spread out his fingers and I heard a small clunk. His hand was big and pale and the webs between his fingers went halfway up to the first knuckle. I felt his eyes on me. When he lifted his hand, still spread out and tense, a knife lay on my desk. A red Swiss army knife.

And the six years vaporized into nothing and I was eleven years old again. I was in a rowboat and everything about that bad summer became enclosed in one moment, when I threw the knife. The summer of being eleven.

That summer we rented a cabin up the coast. It was going to be so good. There was a tree house and a rowboat and Dad would come up every weekend. I slept in a room with bunk beds and a door covered in glued-on seashells and driftwood.

The first morning I woke up early. The birds were loud. I got up quietly and pulled on some clothes and went down to the beach. The rowboat was right there, waiting for me. I rowed around for a while, getting the feel of the oars. There was a thin mist on the surface of the water. And then, as I was lazily drifting in on the tide, there was the sound of a small splash, and a shiny black cannonball head popped out of the mist, a seal. He stared right at me, friendly but quizzical, as if to say, "What kind of a strange seal are you?" He had huge shiny brown eyes and grandfather whiskers. He swam right around the boat once. Then he slipped under the glassy surface and disappeared.

To let a little happiness out, I rowed around the cove like a maniac, like it was some Rowboat Indy 500. When I got back to the cabin, Mom was just getting up. We had hot dogs for breakfast.

That first week I saw the seal every morning. He glided past the boat underwater, on his side or even upside down, fat and sleek. He started to come so close I could almost touch him. He liked to hide in the seaweed. I decided his name was Rollo, because he was so good at rolling over.

"My dad's coming Friday after work," I told Rollo. "And guess what? Friday is my birthday. I'm not going to tell him about you. On Saturday morning I'll surprise him. We'll come out in the boat. We'll be pretty early. My dad is an early riser. So am I. I inherited it."

Dad was late that Friday. We waited and waited. Mom walked up to the phone booth at the corner where the dirt road met the highway. When she came back, her face was like concrete.

But then he came. He arrived at the door holding my cake with the candles already lit. He had parked the car around the curve of the road and snuck up to the house.

"Happy birthday, birthday boy!"

The cake was chocolate with blue icing. The decoration in the middle was a little wooden dog on a stand. In the candlelight it looked like a miniature real dog who was all set to bark and jump up and give me a tiny lick.

I made a wish. I don't remember what it was. What did I wish for before I started to wish for the same thing over and over? I blew out the candles and pulled the dog out of the icing. I pushed the button on the bottom of the stand and he collapsed. I let it go and he jumped back into shape.

"Present time," said Dad, and he set something on the table beside my plate. It was a bright red Swiss army knife.

I picked it up. It was smooth and solid and heavy. I pulled out one stiff shining blade.

"Jerry, don't you think that's a bit dangerous?" said Mom.

"He'll be careful, won't you, pal?" said Dad.

Dad and I looked at all the parts of the knife, the blades and scissors, the corkscrew and screwdriver, the tweezers and toothpick, the tool for taking stones out of horses' hooves. Dad made jokes about me opening bottles of wine and learning to whittle and helping out horses in distress. He got louder and louder and jokier. Mom stopped talking.

When I went to bed I put the knife under my pillow. Later I woke up and heard Mom and Dad arguing. There was yelling and crying. Anger seeped through the wooden wall beside me. I grabbed the knife and put the pillow over my head.

I woke up early the next morning and jumped into my shorts. I put my knife in my pocket. I peeked into Mom and Dad's room. Mom was asleep, huddled into a ball. Dad wasn't there. I ran outside, up the road, around the curve. The car was gone. The dust was soft around my feet.

He didn't say good-bye. He didn't come out in the boat with me. He didn't meet Rollo.

I spent most of that day in the tree house thinking and gouging the wooden planks with the biggest blade of the knife. And I figured it out. They were fighting about the knife. I would just hide it away and then they would forget about it and it would be okay again.

Dad didn't come the next weekend or once again that summer. But still I kept my knife hidden in my pocket, next to the collapsing dog.

Until the day I went out in the rowboat with Laurel.

How did I end up in the rowboat with Laurel? It can't have been my idea.

Mom must have arranged it. Laurel and her family had the next cabin but one. Mom spent a lot of time sitting on their deck, drinking coffee and smoking and talking to Laurel's mother. Mom said how nice it was that Laurel was just my age so that I could have a friend because it must be a bit lonely for me. It wasn't nice at all. I hated Laurel. She looked like a weasel and talked like a grown-up. Besides, I already had a friend, Rollo. I avoided Laurel.

But I guess I got trapped that day.

I don't remember why we were in the boat. But I remember absolutely clearly what happened. I can rerun that tape anytime.

We're floating around in the middle of the cove. I'm letting Laurel row because she has a way of getting what she wants. I take out my knife and she grabs it. She pops the scissors in and out in a way I know is going to break them. She takes the tweezers out and starts tweezing my leg with them. I lunge for them and she throws them back at me and they disappear over the side of the boat. I see them sinking, a little silver light and then they disappear into the murk.

I want to scream and cry and hurt Laurel. But I don't. I hold out my hand for the knife and she gives it to me, slapping it down on my palm. "Here's your stupid old knife." I run my thumb over the hole where the tweezers should be. I pull out the biggest blade and push its point into the side of the rowboat, seeing how hard I can push before it starts to enter the wood. Laurel starts to row again, out toward the mouth of the cove. She doesn't look at me.

"I hear your father's got a new girlfriend." She acts like she's talking to air.

I don't say anything.

"I heard your mom talking to my mom. He's got a new girlfriend. Her name's Carmelle. She's going to have a baby."

"That's not true." I knew it was true. Things added up. The little collapsing dog jumped into shape.

"Oh, grow up," said Laurel. "Just wait. They'll take you aside and say, 'We've grown apart but this isn't your fault.'"

I stuck the knife into the gunwale of the boat.

"They read it in books, you know. How to tell your kids about divorce." She made her voice deep as a dad's. "'We can't live together but we both still love you.'" And then she laughed her weasel laugh.

I didn't think about what I did next. I could not have stopped my hand, which grabbed the knife and pitched it through the air toward Laurel. It missed her by a mile and then everything slowed right down. The knife turned in the blue air and Rollo raised his little cat face above the water. Why was he there? He was never there in the middle of the day. He was only there in the early morning. The knife flew toward that head, oh, so slowly. And then they joined. I saw the red knife sway once in the seal's head just before he dived.

I've told this part like a story. But as I sat at my desk staring at that knife, it didn't come back as a story, but as one moment of feeling, with blue sky and Laurel laughing and the obscenity of that red knife sticking out of the side of that gentle seal head.

The moment came and went as Ron looked at me. I picked up the knife and ran my thumb over where the tweezers would have been. It wasn't as heavy as I remembered. It wasn't as heavy as the memory of that moment.

When I looked up, Ron had walked away. He was standing at the front of the room and everyone was jostling by him. Hester had Don in a hammerlock and was escorting him out the door. I seemed to have collapsing-dog legs. Ron turned back to look at me and slowly took off his cap. His hair was black, thick, and very short. And just above his temple there was a white line. Some guys do that. They shave patterns into their hair. Then he smiled at me, friendly and quizzical as if to say, "What kind of weird seal are you?" And something inside me, something hard and heavy, went fuzzy at the edges and started to melt away. He turned and walked out the door.

Ron wasn't in school on Monday. Or Tuesday. I asked Mrs. F. about him. She consulted her much-erased class register. "He transferred out," she said. "A single day's attendance. That's the record, the shortest stay I've ever had from a student. I guess he didn't like your face, Curtis." She smiled and the members of the core community snorted and made rude noises. I thought about what it must be like to push through air on two legs, air heavy with gravity, when your body remembers sliding and diving and rolling through the slippery sea.

The knife. I think I'll give it to Stevie when I see him tonight. Dad dropped by on the weekend. He has a beard now. We had a careful conversation. He talked about Stevie. He told me that the little guy is nervous about starting kindergarten. Apparently Carmelle asked him if he was looking forward to school and he said, "No, I'm looking sideways." Dad said Stevie talks about me all the time and really wants to meet me.

So I'll go. And I'll give Stevie the knife. He could probably use a present, a heavy present to keep in his pocket. Sometimes it's good to have something to hang on to. And sometimes it's good to give things away.

HAPPEN

I was sitting in Grandad's kitchen trying to figure out which way the world turns. When Dad and I drove out here from Ontario, it started to seem, especially around day three on the prairies, that we weren't really moving, that the earth was just turning under us. But was that the right direction? I spun an apple on the table and pretended I was the sun. I thought about time zones. But my brain just couldn't get it.

Which confirms my suspicion that I'm not smart. I used to be smart. Or maybe I was never smart. Maybe I was just nice, so teachers liked me and gave me good marks. But last year I stopped being smart. Or nice. Last year was the pits.

I was glad to be at Grandad's. Dad and I were here to help him get ready to move into town, from his old house to a condominium. I was glad to be away.

Dad came into the kitchen and drank from the tap. "It's a hot one. I'm nearly done out there. The stuff that's going to Rob is all packed in the trailer. I'd like to leave right after lunch, hit the road by one or so, make it to Rob and Louise's by dinner."

"Anything you want me to do?"

"Can't think of anything. Ask Grandad."

Grandad was in the shed sorting nails and smoking. "I'm just going to take a small selection. Might come in handy. They have a workshop in the basement of that aquarium place."

"Condominium, Grandad."

He winked at me. "Whatever. What are you up to?"

"Don't know."

"Want to pick some blackberries? There's lots across the road. Be nice to take some to Louise."

"Okay."

"We'll get you the kit then."

From a shelf he pulled paint-spattered blue coveralls. I pulled them on over my shorts and tank top. He knelt down to roll up the legs for me and I looked through his hair to his shiny head, like an egg. He found me a cap and then he tied a rope to the handles of a yellow plastic bucket and placed it around my neck. "Leaves both hands free for picking." Finally he handed me an aluminum step stool. "There you go, all set for serious picking."

I looked like some crazed house-painter. But I didn't have far to go. I crossed the road and scrambled down and up the dry ditch. I looked around. Near the edge the berries were picked over and dusty. But I pushed my way into the tangle, invincible in my thermonuclear protection outfit. The bushes closed in around me and I was surrounded by berries, hanging thick and black. I picked and ate and picked and saved. The plunk of berries falling into the bucket became softer as the bucket filled up. I pushed farther into the bush. I hardly had to reach for the berries, there were so many of them.

The sun beat down and there was a distant hum of bees. My fingers turned purple. Maybe I would just stay here and live on blackberries and not go home. Escape fantasy number forty-seven. Half a continent away, hidden in a blackberry patch, I wouldn't have to figure out what to do about Alan.

Alan. The boyfriend. Funny, popular, good-looking, likes me, not a show-off. Nice to adoring seven-year-old girls of whom my sister, Angie, is an excellent example. And very together. Once, in biology class he said "testicle" by mistake when he meant "tentacle." The class went berserk, especially the lunkoids in the back seats. I would have blushed purple and died. But Alan just laughed along. He's kind of short. I think he figured out how to be kind of short and not get beat up.

Carrie and Lisa say I'm *so* lucky. And I tell myself they're right. What I don't tell them, and hardly tell myself, is that sometimes when I'm with Alan I feel like a total phony. Like I'm just playing along with the boyfriend game, painting by numbers. Choose one person and concentrate on him exclusively; fill in all the green areas of the picture. Accumulate information about this person and discuss him with your friends; fill in all the red areas of the picture. Arrange for the subject to find out about your interest; paint in those yellow bits. Careful! Don't go over the lines! And so on until you have a tidy little still life that you can frame and put on the wall. It's easy to make it all happen. But why? And I wonder if everybody is doing that, inventing. Who would tell you? You don't see that question in *Teen Scene Advisor*.

Alan invited me to come with him and his family to their cottage this summer. I knew if I went I would end up pushing him off a dock or something. It's that look, that needy look. It makes me want to run away. I said I couldn't because I had to come on this trip with my dad. But I guess I didn't act sorry enough because he knew. He looked hurt and it was like when I crunched Angie's hand in the car door by mistake. And then because he looked hurt

I got mad at him for making me feel that way. Which is not a nice thing to do. Which is why I don't think I'm nice anymore. Or smart. And why I keep thinking of escape plans.

The bucket filled up almost by magic and the rope around my neck was starting to hurt. Enough. It must be nearly time to go back anyway. And then I looked up and saw, just out of reach, a fistful of the biggest, blackest berries glowing in the sun, the best last berries to pick. I opened the step stool and tried to find some level ground.

I climbed up the three steps and the berries fell into my hand. I glanced over the tangle of branches and there was a garden just beyond. Shrubs, vegetables in rows, flowers of every color. I leaned out but I couldn't see a house or a street or the edge of the garden. The stool began to tip and I jumped off. A thorny branch got me on the way down. I sucked the little beads of blood off the back of my hand. I wanted to be in that garden.

I took off my bucket and left it at the base of the step stool. Then I turned up the collar of the coveralls, pulled my hands up into the sleeves, and backed through the tangle of bushes. Thorns tore at my clothes and one branch grabbed my hat. I left it, pushed through, and fell backward onto a smooth lawn.

I looked around quickly to see if anyone had seen me, but the garden was still and empty. I pulled apart the snaps on the coveralls and stepped free of them. The sound of running water made me realize how thirsty I was. I followed the sound to a small stream, running over smooth rocks. The banks were covered in moss and they curved over into the stream like blankets tucked into a bed. I lay down on the softness and stuck my face in the water. I opened my eyes and a tiny silver fish slid by. I surfaced and remembered about the time.

Just until I dry off, I told myself, then I'll go back. A swallow swooped by, low to the ground, a flash of violet green. He landed in a hedge. I followed him, shaking my wet hands in the air. The hedge, shoulder high, was dotted with small red and purple bell-shaped flowers. I crouched down to look up at them. They were bright and clear, glowing almost. Maybe my eyeballs had gotten washed in the stream.

A face appeared over the hedge. "Hello."

I tipped backward onto my bum. The face laughed. "Didn't mean to startle you." Black hair. Laughing white teeth. I scrambled to my feet with the grace of a moose.

"Sorry. Sorry, I was picking berries and I was thirsty. I'm just going."

"Don't go," said the face. "We enjoy visitors in the garden."

"Do you live here?"

A nod. "Off and on. Stay, I'll come around." There was something in the eyes that drew a little circle around the two of us.

I watched the shirt retreat. I stepped back to better see the flashes of white through the hedge. I stumbled again. It was as though my brain had tilted slightly. Was the face a boy or a girl? I shook my head. What did it matter? Get a grip. Was that the very most important thing about a person? Was I becoming like Carrie and Lisa with a specially invented self-for-boys? I hate that.

The white shirt appeared around the edge of the hedge and after a few steps I knew. It wasn't the clothes, big white shirt and gray pants. It wasn't the hair, short flat curls. It was something about the movement.

She ran up to me and smiled. "Come on," she said. "I'll show you things."

She spun away. I followed. The garden was crowded and

bright, a 3-D kaleidoscope of colors and shapes. The girl was always just ahead of me, running around curving daisy-dotted grassy paths, disappearing through gates and hedges.

I lost track of her for a minute near a wall of giant nodding sunflowers. She appeared beside me holding cherries. She hung two pairs over my ears. Then she laughed and ran away again. As I ran after her the cherries brushed my cheeks lightly, like finger-tips. They were the smell of summer.

She finally stopped at the edge of a pond. She was sitting on a large flat rock when I caught up with her. She laid her finger across her lips and then raised her hand, palm-side up, to the level of her face and kept it there, motionless. My heart was beating hard from the run and we sat so silently that I thought she might be able to hear it. A yellow butterfly appeared from nowhere and landed on her hand. It opened and closed its wings twice and then lay open on her hand like a book. She tilted her hand slightly toward me. The yellow wings were edged with bright neon pink. They trembled slightly.

"Pink-edged sulfur," she said.

"How did you get it to land on you?"

She gave a small shrug. "If you know the names of things, you see them, and then they come to you."

The butterfly lifted off and flew away over the pond.

We flipped over onto our stomachs. We ate the cherry ear-rings. I stared out over the water, blue in the sun and black in the shadows of the overhanging trees. A bird swooped down, touching the water with its wings, leaving a set of hypnotic interconnecting circles. Near my face a bug, with long legs thin as pencil lines, walked across the surface of the water. I started to think about birds soaring in air and fish diving in water and humans walking on surfaces like water bugs.

The girl rolled over and jumped up. "Want to see the best place?"

She walked beside me this time, around the curve of the pond, past a blanket of water lilies to a large bush covered in white blossoms. The overhanging branches made a curtain. She pulled it aside.

When Lisa and Carrie and I were little, we used to make forts out of chairs and blankets. It was safe and private.

We lay down with our heads against the trunk, like two spokes of a wheel. We looked up through white blossoms and black branches to a watercolor blue sky. The air smelled like oranges.

"Look," she said.

I looked where she was looking. "What?"

She reached over and turned my face slightly. She pointed. There, floating between black branches, was the moon—a thin, white tissue-paper moon.

The touch of her fingers was still on my face. I lay very still, feeling the tickle of leaves on the back of my knees, breathing in the orange-scented air, and knowing the exact shape and size of the sun-puddled space between our two bodies. I was filled with a rock of certainty around which flowed a stream of questions.

When I was a kid I had this book of *Gulliver's Travels*. On the cover was a picture of Gulliver lying on the ground, surrounded by little people and tied down with rope. He didn't look that scared. In fact, he looked like he could break those thread-thin ropes anytime he chose to. That was me under those white blossoms, unmoving, pinned down to the warm dirt, and big, big inside, like a giant.

I lay there for a minute, or a day. And then it was like one of those little people marched up to my ear and yelled, "Dad! Lunch!

Remember?" And then I did remember and I had to go back.

I didn't have to tell her. She looked at me, into me, holding me with her eyes, green eyes flecked with gold. "You'll be back here again?"

Well, not really. We live on the other side of the country and Grandad is moving and there would be no reason . . .

But I didn't need to explain. That wasn't what she meant.

"Yes," I said, "I will."

We walked back to the blackberry wall. I felt like a moon walker about to float free with every step. My coveralls lay in a heap. I slipped them on. They smelled of smoke, like Grandad.

"Good-bye, then."

"Good-bye."

"You go first."

"No, you."

My mouth couldn't stop smiling. "On three, then."

"All right. One, two . . . stop!" She jumped away a few steps and reached up into the leaves of a nearby tree. She pulled down a peach and put it in my hand. "Three."

I pushed through the brambles backward and then I cheated and stuck my head back through. She was running, swinging around trees and jumping over flower beds. There was a flash of white and then she was gone.

The berry bucket and the stool were there. I knew I should hurry. But the peach smelled too good, sun-warmed. I bit into it, letting the juice run down my chin and over my hand. I was going to be hours late.

But when I got back, Dad was just tying the tarp over the trailer. He helped himself to a handful of berries. "Heaven," he said.

Grandad was still sorting nails. I grabbed his wrist and looked at his watch. Ten past twelve.

"Yes," he said, "lunchtime. What's this in your hair?" He gently smoothed a strand of bramble tangle and held up a white blossom. He sniffed it. "Mock orange, your grandmother's favorite."

For lunch we had clam chowder, mandarin orange segments, refried beans, and sardines. "No point packing canned goods," said Grandad.

"I found a garden," I said.

"Did you?" said Grandad. "You must have gone clear over to the other side of the vacant lot. That'll be one of the gardens of the properties on Arcadia Estates, damn fool name for a bunch of jerry-rigged houses. Have you ever noticed that they name these housing developments for what they have destroyed? The Cedars, that'll be for the cedars they chopped down. What kind of a garden? No, let me guess. Concrete, bark chips, and two rhododendrons."

"No, it had flowers and fruit trees. And a stream. I ate a peach."

"A peach? You won't get peaches for another month, unless they're growing them in a greenhouse. Never heard of that."

The weight of it in my hand. Breaking through the furriness to smoothness. Sticky chin. I did remember it. But it was sliding away. And there had been no greenhouse. Grandad finished his coffee. "I'll probably be drinking cappuccino from now on, seeing as how I'm going to be a yuppie, living in a condom."

"Father! Condo, not condom."

Grandad looked sideways at me. "Whatever. Now you better get on out of here. Have you got everything? Oh, by the way, Gus, you know that vise out on the workbench. I've been thinking that Rob could use that, too. You unhitch it and take it along with you, will you?"

Dad sighed, looked pointedly at the clock and went out the kitchen door.

Grandad went to an open box in the corner. "I've got something for you." He took out a black leather folder and handed it to me. "Reading matter for the trip. Some treasures from your grandmother."

He gave me a tight hug that trembled a bit. "Come see me on your own sometime. Leave the old man at home. Bring a friend. There's always room for you at the terrarium."

"Condominium, you old faker."

"Oh, is that it? Whatever."

I waited until we hit the highway before I opened the folder. Inside was a jumble of old cards and drawings, some yellowed newspaper clippings, and folded scraps of paper. I pulled out a handful and spread them out on my knees. There was a big lop-sided construction paper heart, faded to pale pink. "To Mommy, from Angus." Above the words was a drawing of a mean-looking car with giant fins.

"Hey, Dad, look. Did you make this valentine?"

Dad glanced over and grinned. "I used to love drawing cars."

Halfway down the pile was a thick cream-colored envelope. When I opened it some dried rose petals fell onto my lap. I slid out the card. On the front it said, in Grandad's pointed writing, "For Anna, on our anniversary." Inside was a message written like a poem.

This is the garden of lost and found
Night and day
Spring and fall
Dawn and dusk

Sun and moon
Waking, sleeping, and dreaming.

This is the garden of growing and grown
Planting and picking
Of blossom and fruit.

You cannot find this garden by searching
You can only happen upon it.
We live in this garden
You and I.

I read it twice. I picked up the rose petals and arranged them over the words. Then I closed the card and slid it back into the envelope and put everything back into the folder.

Sun and moon.

"Dad?"

"Uh-huh."

"How come you sometimes see the moon in the day?"

"It has to do with the phases. The moon actually rises about noon in the first quarter. But of course it is very pale so we don't often see it."

"What phase is the moon in now?"

"Just gone full. Behaving normally and rising and setting at night."

I stared down the road, holding the folder tight. He had been there. Grandad. Sun and moon. Discovery and decision. Making it happen and letting it happen. Both. All. Everything.

I thought about the colors of the garden. Dusty yellow and glass-clear pink, the blue-black of water, her green eyes flecked with gold. More complicated than paint-by-numbers. More real.

The music on the radio, some kind of fiddle thing, suddenly matched exactly the rhythm of the dotted center line of the road. I cranked up the volume to the max. "Right on," said Dad and power-rolled down all the windows. I reached out and rested my hand on the rearview mirror. The wind rolled across my arm like water. We drove toward home, in the direction of the turning world.

CHECK

Today is Thursday. It's the day I go to visit my mother. I go once every two weeks. Dad picks me up after school and drives me to her apartment. But he doesn't come in. It seems to work better that way.

Sometimes Dad can't get away from work early so I have time to kill at school. Usually I hang out at the library, but today I decided to act like a normal teenager. So I walked down the street to the mall.

Halloween is over so the mall is decorated for Christmas. This year they've gone in for a gingerbread theme. Gingerbread persons are everywhere, looming, splayed against the windows of the drugstore, the knife shop, Vitamin World, the jewelry store/body-piercing salon, and the eighteen thousand shoe stores. I walked the length of the mall and thought about symbolism. "Run, run as fast as you can. You can't catch me, I'm the gingerbread man." We create these people who look like children, although we call them men and women, we bake them in the oven until they are rigid and dead, and then we bite their heads off. We're doing symbolism in our English class. Usually I'm not that great in English. But I really like symbolism.

At the far end of the mall, tucked away behind a staircase, is an oversize chessboard, marble tiles laid in contrasting colors. The players, mostly old men, use knee-high chess pieces. The Muzak doesn't make it around the corner. It is the most unmall part of the mall.

I sat down on one of the benches that ring the board and noticed that the area had remained a gingerbread-free zone. There was a game in progress. Black was a grandfather type. Gray mustache, cardigan with a tie. White was younger, university age. Glasses, computer look. He seemed to be cleaning up. They were both enclosed by that dome of concentration that surrounds chess players.

Beyond them on the opposite bench was an old woman in a dark green track suit. She had white hair and a wrinkled face. She smiled at me, raised her eyebrows, and gave a little wave. Did I know her? She bounced up from her seat, fast-walked around the edge of the chessboard, and slid in beside me. "Hello, Chloe, how are you doing?"

I searched my brain. Was she somebody's grandmother? Was she one of those people on the block who hires Ryan to cut their grass? Not a clue. I'd have to go with nonspecific friendliness.

"Fine, thanks!"

"So, what do you think? Looks to me like the young man is in trouble. A knight on the rim is very dim."

"Pardon?"

"Never leave your knight on the edge, Toots. He loses half his maneuverability. This young man, he started out very well, very aggressive. That's good. But he has lost control of the center of the board. Look."

Black was taking a long time to make his move. He strolled

around the board with a small smile on his lips.

There was a kind of vibration from the woman beside me, not an old-person tremble, but something like an electric hum. I glanced sideways, half expecting to see a blue static crackle in the air around her.

She let out her breath, like someone blowing out a candle, as Black moved his bishop with a graceful swing.

"Beautiful, it's a fork."

I was lost. "What's a fork?"

"Attacking two of your opponent's pieces at the same time with just one of yours. Makes your opponent very nervous." She chuckled. "Ha! That's got him on the hop. I'd say that was the turning point. You play, don't you?"

I shook my head. "I know how the pieces move but that's all. I've never played a game."

Which wasn't quite true. I did play a game of chess once. My own game.

It started when she woke us up in the middle of the night. Daddy was away on a sales trip. She was laughing and singing. She picked up Ryan and tickled him and polkaed him around the room. She got us dressed and she stuffed some things in our backpacks. "Holiday time," she said.

I was barely awake. "No, it isn't."

"Oh, Chloe, don't be so literal. We're making up our own holiday. We'll call it . . . Christihalloweaster." Ryan giggled.

When we were little, Mommy was good at playing. She made up silly songs. She painted flowers on our toenails, Ryan's too. She was the only mom I ever saw on a trampoline. Once my friend Crystal asked me if my mother was a real grown-up. But that night the playing didn't feel good. My clothes were scratchy and cold. I wanted to be in my pajamas again.

She put us in the car. We were only about five minutes from home when Ryan said, "Where's my corner?"

Ryan's corner was what was left of his baby blanket. It was just a grubby yellow rag but he needed it. We could have gone back.

But Mommy just laughed. "Oh, Ryan, sweetie, you don't need your corner. We're leaving all that behind us. All those *things,* they're just a trap."

Ryan started to cry. I pulled some fuzz off my sweater and gave it to him. He held it against his cheek, put his thumb in his mouth, and went to sleep.

Mom was acting very happy. She started to sing songs from musicals. Her big, clear voice filled every corner of the car. Between songs she talked about the good times we were going to have. "We're going to see color, children. Bright color, not all this gray, gray, gray all the time."

We stopped for gas. She was jokey with the gas-station man. He called her Babe. I hated him.

"Is Daddy coming?"

"If he ever wants to leave his gray little office and his gray little life, sure he can come." Ryan slept in his booster seat, snoring his little-boy snores. But I was wide awake. I pulled my seat belt over my face and chewed on it. I thought about school. The next day the principal was going to wear his pajamas to school. He said he would if the grade threes read enough at the readathon and we did, so he was going to. "Will I go to school tomorrow?"

"Oh, Chloe, *life* is a school. I hope you're not going to be boring about school."

We came to a bright empty city. To a hotel. A man dressed up like a wooden soldier took the car away and we went through revolving doors with gold on them. Mommy was carrying Ryan in one arm. With her other hand she swung her bag as we crossed the wide lobby. She joked with the men at the desk and they called her Madam. We went up in an elevator with mirrors. Mommy pretended to do ballet. Ryan laughed. We had two big rooms with a door between. The beds were as big as two beds. There was a little fridge full of pop and chips and chocolate bars. There was a phone in the bathroom and free toothbrushes in plastic bags, but Mommy didn't make us brush our teeth. Ryan came into my bed later.

The next morning when we woke up, there was a wagon in the room with breakfast on it. Chocolate buns and orange juice in glasses with hats on them. Ryan and I ate and Mommy drank coffee and talked on the phone. She phoned Auntie Eunice and Mrs. Singh our neighbor, and Paula, her friend in Australia. She told everyone what a good time we were having and then she made us say hello. Ryan jumped on the bed and I asked when we were going home and Mommy said where did I learn to be such a wet blanket.

When I think about that day now, I see big white napkins in the restaurant where we ate cream puffs shaped like swans. I see a long escalator with mirrors on either side, mirrors that make us look as though we have golden shadows. I see a huge box of Lego, the set that has windows and doors and motors, enough Lego to make a whole world, a box so big that Ryan can't even get his arms around it. I see a velvet jumper. It comes in emerald green, a blue that is almost purple, and the reddest red. I can't decide which I like the best so Mommy buys all three. I see Ryan sucking his thumb until it is chapped. I see Mommy laughing.

All day, laughing. Until we got to the hotel gift shop. It was after dinner. Mommy said we could go swimming in the hotel pool. We were walking through the lobby on the way to the elevator when Mommy saw a polar bear sculpture in the window of this store. She wanted it. She bought it. Then she said to us, "Have anything you want. Go on. Pick. Anything at all."

Ryan pulled on Mommy's hand. "I want to go in the pool."

His voice had an almost-whine. Mommy stopped smiling.

I quickly pointed to the first thing I saw. It was on a low glass shelf, a box full of little velvet-lined compartments. In each compartment was an ornament made of shiny stone and decorated with a dark green jewel. Emeralds, my birthstone. There was a green set on one side of the box and a white set on the other. They looked cozy in their little perfectly shaped beds.

"We'll take that chess set," said Mommy.

"Really, Madam?" The clerk looked surprised.

"Yes, really. Do you have a problem with that?"

"Not at all. It's just that it is a rather expensive item for a child."

Mom took out her charge card and snapped it down on the glass counter. "My children deserve the best. And I fail to see where it is any of your business." Her face went hard.

All the way up in the elevator she talked about the saleslady. "Snobby little snip." By the time we got to our room, she didn't like the hotel anymore.

Ryan was pulling off his clothes. "If there's a big slide and a little slide, can I go on the big slide? Please? I'm not a-scared and I can do the dog paddle."

Mom threw her packages onto the bed. "You spend all this money and they treat you like shit. We're not going swimming."

Ryan threw himself on the floor. "You said. You promised. I want to."

Mom dragged him to his feet and slapped him.

Everything stopped. Our mother never says bad words or slaps us.

It was like she forgot who we were.

"All right, Chloe. I'm going out. You take care of your brother. Give him a bath and make sure he's down by eight."

That's what Mommy said to our baby-sitter. I was only nine. I wasn't old enough to baby-sit. She shouldn't be going out and leaving us alone. I didn't know how to even start to say this.

She locked the little fridge. "No more junk food. It's bad for your teeth. I won't be late."

Then she left.

Ryan was looking at me with huge eyes. I couldn't think of what to do but what she told me to do. I let Ryan wear his bathing suit in the bath but the bathtub had a funny plug. I couldn't make the water stay in. I did make him brush his teeth. We didn't have any books for a bedtime story so I read the first-aid instructions in the front of the phone book. We read about the carotid artery and foreign bodies in the eye. I read the whole of "bleeding from a protruding object," but Ryan was still lying with wide-awake eyes.

"Do you want the last song?" I asked. Mommy always sang the same song to Ryan last thing at night. She sang it to me when I was little. Her grandmother sang it to her. It had a good-sad tune and words that didn't really make sense.

Ryan nodded and pulled the covers over his head. I started:

Hovan, hovan, garry-a-go,
Garry-a-go, Garry-a-go.
Hovan, hovan, garry-a-go,
I've lost my darling baby-o.

I've lost him out in the mist on the moor,
Mist on the moor, mist on the moor.
I've lost him out in the mist on the moor,
Oh, where's my darling baby-o.

Them that's in it will carry him home,
Carry him home, carry him home.
Them that's in it will carry him home,
Safe to my arms, my baby-o.

My voice was thin. It didn't fill the room. Ryan was quiet and I sat beside him on the bed. I remembered how the last song used to make me feel, strong and safe, a bold explorer out on the moor, safely carried home by the mysterious "them that's in it," a flock of angel/fairy/birds in my mind.

I gently pulled the covers away from Ryan's face. He was asleep. I turned out the light and took my lobby shop present into the bathroom. I gathered all the big fat white towels and piled them in the bathtub for a cushion. Then I got into the tub with my present. I opened the tiny gold catch on the box and unwrapped each piece. I arranged them on the edge of the tub. They were smooth and cool, just like the bathtub. Their emeralds glittered in the bright bathroom light. I had no idea what they were. I gave them names—horses and castles, knob-heads and pointy-heads and fancy-heads. I made families. The castles married the pointy-heads. The fancy-heads married each other. They had a lot of knob-head children. The girls were green and the boys were white. They all had ponies. I put the ponies out to pasture on the soap dish. Then I put the children to bed under facecloth blankets, with their heads on soap pillows.

That's where I was when Dad came. Mrs. Singh had traced the number and phoned him. He just scooped us up. He didn't bother with any of our things. In his car was Ryan's corner.

Mom came home again but she didn't stay for long. I sometimes miss those little jeweled dolls.

Now I go to see her. Ryan won't go. Sometimes it's okay. We do the crossword puzzle in the paper or watch old Monty Python videos. Then we order in pizza or Chinese. She has good ideas. For my last birthday she bought me an umbrella and painted it with fabric paints, black on the outside and a brilliant blue with puffy clouds on the inside. It was beautiful, but by the time she gave it to me she didn't like it. "It didn't work," she said as I unwrapped it.

She's like that, like a half-deflated balloon. Nothing is good. The place the paperboy leaves the paper, the checkout system at the public library, the woman at work who used to be her friend until she got so snobby, the way the city prunes the boulevard trees. Nothing is ever really right.

The most not-right thing is me. My posture is bad: "Don't slouch like that." I don't speak properly: "Real is *not* an adverb." I'm fat: "What are you eating?" I wear the wrong clothes: "Someone with your sallow complexion should never wear yellow."

I know what it is about. I've read the book and talked to the family counselor. I know she's just trying to be a mother. I know she has an illness. I know about the medication. But knowing doesn't always help. Those words glue onto your mind. You look at yourself in the mirror and you see a fat, slouching, sallow person.

Once, when she seemed a bit happy, I tried to get her to sing.

"Mom? Remember that song you used to sing about Sally Spunky?"

She shook her head. "I don't remember."

"Come on! *'Sally Spunky dressed all in green, sent rude pictures on the fax machine.'* You used to sing it to me and Ryan. Did you make it up?"

"Probably."

"Because I've been trying to remember what goes with the slug verse." I started to sing. *"Sally Spunky wears a slug for a hat, slug for a hat . . .* Mom?"

And then she just turned on me. *"I don't remember*, Chloe. Just lay off."

So now I don't talk about anything from before, like Dad or his family or the neighborhood. I don't disagree with her, ever. I dress plainly and don't wear makeup or change my hair. I don't do anything surprising. I try to be as smooth as a knob-head. It is my Thursday self.

The old woman in green gave a single clap. "Right on!" I looked over at the board. In the time I had been remembering, there had been major casualties on both sides. Black was just removing his own pawn from the board and replacing it with a queen. He was allowing himself a little smile.

"What's up?" I asked.

"Pawn promotion," she said. "If you manage to get your pawn all the way to the eighth rank, to the opposite end of the board, it can turn into anything you like, usually a queen. Once you have two queens, you're sitting pretty, of course. Two ladies who get to go in whatever direction they choose and as far as they like."

She turned to me. Her eyes were a deep, clear, brilliant blue.

And for just a split second I almost recognized her. Like a word on the tip of my tongue, her face was on the tip of my mind. But recognition skittered away as I ran after it.

"You just keep moving ahead. You survive all those hazards and then you are transformed." She smiled. "It makes a lovely endgame."

"You mean it's over?"

"Just watch."

White was staring hard at the board. Then he went sort of limp, reached out, and tipped his king over. It made a little *tock* sound on the marble. He gave a total body shrug, arms out, palms up. He smiled and then he and Black shook each other by the hands and elbows.

"Did Black have that all figured out ahead?"

"Not really, you can't play too far in advance. Because you can't predict your opponent. Every move it's a new game. The trick is to be able to abandon one strategy and devise another when things change."

"You sure know a lot about chess."

She smiled. "Ah, I've followed chess all my long-legged life, which is longer than I care to say. I'm one of the old ones, as you know."

We watched while Black and White packed away the chess pieces. I wanted to help, just to touch those plain smooth wooden shapes. Then, very quietly, the old woman beside me started to hum and to tap her fingers lightly on her leg.

"Hovan, hovan, garry-a-go . . ."

It was the last song. Nobody else knows that song. As I turned to her with a question with no words, she hummed a flourish on the last note and touched my arm for a second.

"Bless you," she said, and she stood up and walked away, her purse swinging.

"See you," I said to the retreating flash of green, "and . . . thanks." There was a lingering sense of someone still on the bench beside me. A shape. It faded.

I'm walking back down the mall, down the marble-tiled floor. The squares are just the size for human chess pieces. I'm careful not to step on the cracks. Right at the end of the mall, facing me, is the body-piercing shop, "no appointment necessary." Pawn promotion. If I were a knob-head (okay, pawn), all I would have to do is keep on going straight ahead, cheered on by the ranks of gingerbread, and at the end I could be a queen. I look at my watch and reach up to touch the side of my nose. A jeweled queen. A bold fancy-head who gets to go in whatever direction she wants.

GORE

Twins have a very special bond. Together from their earliest moments of consciousness, they are true soul mates. Linked by feelings of deep kinship and love, mutually attuned with an almost magic sensitivity, they often feel like two halves of the same person.

Twins separated at birth who meet as adults often discover amazing coincidences in their lives. They both have wives named Linda and sons called Hamish. At their weddings both of their best men wore kilts. They both have Maine coon cats and use an obscure Finnish brand of aftershave. This proves that the twin relationship is one of the strongest in the world, overriding individual personality and the forces of upbringing and environment.

Horse patooties.

Soul mates? Sometimes I can't believe that Lucas and I are in the same family, much less twins. In fact, there have been times when I've wondered if Lucas and I are even of the same species. I'm pretty much a basic Homo sapiens. Lucas is more like an unevolved thugoid. I've heard that there are some photos of twins in the womb that show them hugging. If someone had taken a photo of Lucas and me in there, I'll bet dollars to doughnuts it would have shown him bashing me on the head.

Lucas must have grabbed all the good nutrition in there, too, because he's a lot bigger, faster, and stronger than me. I don't stand a chance on the bashing, kicking, running away, immobilizing-your-opponent-in-a-half-nelson front. As the years have passed, my two areas of superior firepower, an extensive vocabulary and a gift for voice impersonation, have sometimes proved inadequate. I have been forced to take up psychological warfare.

Lucas attacks without provocation. The other day, for example, I'm sitting reading. I finally got the new R. L. Tankard out of the library and it is extremely choice. There's this girl and she has a baby-sitting job in this glam apartment building, on the twenty-sixth floor. When she arrives the baby is already asleep so she hasn't actually seen it. She's watching TV in a darkened room and she thinks she hears a noise from the baby.

> She muted the TV for a minute and in the sudden silence she heard the noise again, but louder. It was a heavy wet noise, like the sound of a big piece of raw meat being flung to the floor. She stared at the door to the nursery. It was outlined in a thin band of crepuscular light. She stood up and, with her heart pounding in her ears, she approached the room . . .

Isn't that excellent? I read it again. Sometimes I like to do that with R. L. Tankard, slow it down by reading the best parts twice before I turn the page. "Crepuscular." I roll the word around in my mouth like a hard candy. Who cares what it means. ". . . like a big piece of raw meat being flung to the floor." Choice.

Then, WHAP! Lucas leans over the back of the chair, rips the book from my hands, runs into the bathroom, and slams the door. I'm after him in a second, but of course by the time I get there he has it locked. I learned years ago that you can click open our bathroom door with a knife. I learned this about two minutes after Lucas learned that you can wedge the bathroom door shut by pulling open the top drawer of the vanity. I kick the door. "Give me my book back, you grommet-head."

"Make me."

I just hate that, the way Lucas can sound so smug. If possible I would appeal to higher authority. I have no shame about finking, whining, telling, etc., when it comes to Lucas. I use whatever counterweapons I have at my disposal. With Lucas as a brother, it is sometimes necessary to have referees. I'm not ashamed to stand behind an adult peacekeeping force. Lucas regards this as an act of cowardice and wimpiness. He tries to shame me. "Why don't you run to Mommy?" But I don't care. I figure it is like some small but extremely valuable country calling on the United Nations when attacked by an aggressor. Unfortunately, in this case, the peacekeeping forces are out at Mega-Foods doing the Saturday shop.

I try to plan a strategy. At least it keeps my mind off what is happening behind the door of that baby's room, in that crepuscular light. The carrot or the stick? Or, to put it another way, the chocolate cheesecake or the uzi? I could try the chocolate cheesecake of false bribery. Such as, "Lucas just give me my book and I'll do your poop-scooping in the backyard this week." This technique has lost its effectiveness through overuse, however. Even Lucas, microbrain that he is, doesn't fall for that one anymore.

So what about the uzi. "Lucas if you don't give me back my book this minute, I'm going to tell Dad that you . . ."—what? I've used up the fact that Lucas was the one who let the rabbit into Mom's office, where it ate through her modem cord. I've already gotten my mileage out of the time he tried to photocopy his bum on the photocopier at the public library. I've used up everything I know about Lucas's sins, crimes, misdemeanors, and shady dealings.

I collapse on the couch in despair. I am a stealth bomber with no aviation fuel. I am a pioneer with no powder for my musket. I am a merry man (well, okay, merry woman) with an empty quiver. I am weaponless.

Not quite.

"Rats. Lucas, there's someone at the door. I'll get it but I'm warning you, Lucas, if you're not out of there by the time I get back, you're toast."

"Yeah, with peanut butter."

I run to the door. The doorbell gives three loud blats.

"Just a minute. Coming!"

I open the door. There are two, no, three of them. The faces are hooded and I only catch a glimpse, but it is enough to make me step back in horror, as though a huge hand has given me a push. This is my first mistake, leaving me a split second too late to push the door shut. They are inside. They are silent.

"Hey, hold it, you can't do that. Get out of here. Help!"

I pull myself together and try to fool them. "Dad!"

The front door clicks quietly shut behind them. I race around the corner and fall against the bathroom door. I strain to hear.

Nothing.

"Lucas," I yell-whisper.

Lucas's bored voice makes its way out of the bathroom. "Forget it, Amy, you're not fooling anybody."

"Lucas, I mean it. Let me in. Please. Those faces. They're not . . . aagh." A shadow falls across me. I grab the doorknob and screw my eyes shut.

The first thing is the smell. The fetid stench. The noxious reek. It is the smell of something dead, sweet and rotten. It rolls through the air like a huge wave, breaking over my head, flowing into my mouth and nose until it becomes a taste. I am drowning. I gasp, dragging the air painfully into my lungs.

"Very dramatic, Lady Macbeth."

I find a voice. "Lucas, can't you smell it?"

Lucas giggles and flushes the toilet. "Now I can't."

Then something ice-cold and soft and damp fixes itself around my wrist like a bracelet and begins to pull my fingers away from the door. I hold on, unable to talk, unable to breathe.

And then the voice. The voice is dry and white as paper. "Come with us, we need you. We need your being."

A cold sweat breaks out over my entire body. I grab at the door one last time as my slippery fingers slide off the knob. I grasp at anything. My fingernails scratch across the shiny surface. The door rattles.

"Lucas!"

Lucas laughs.

The thing moves me to the living room. Not roughly. Like a powerful, persistent, and silent wind. I force my eyes open but I can't seem to focus. The room is shimmering like a mirage on a hot road. I am lying on the floor and the ceiling is pulsing slowly. The strong crepuscular wind pushes me to the floor. I am pinned, paralyzed, frozen with terror. My heartbeat pounds in my ears.

The paper voice is louder. "Eat. Of. Our. Food." Each word is a little island of sound, a pebble dropped into a pool.

The ceiling disappears and a face looms above me. A smooth white mask, skin stretched across sharp bones. Bright yellow eyes that stare unblinking, like a baby or a reptile. Thick, shiny brown hair. The echo of the smell of decay. I feel something being held to my lips. I lock my jaw and squeeze my lips shut.

The voice is louder, booming. "Eat. Of. Our. Food."

I see movement in the shiny brown hair. Movement that ceases the moment I look directly at it. I want to close my eyes but my eyelids are stiff and wooden. The movement increases. Shiny, brown, undulating, dancing like a thing alive.

Or many things alive.

Pink rat eyes. A scream consumes me, vomiting up from every part of my body. And into my open mouth falls a greasy, slimy gobbet of ooze. I flail my head from side to side and try to spit it out, but it turns into a thick, viscous, glutinous, sticky liquid that coats my mouth, rises up the back of my nose, and clings to my teeth. I retch. I gag.

The mask floats once more above me. Its smoothness has now exploded into a cobweb of wrinkles, an old crazed china plate. The hair has turned dead-rat gray. Beads of milky liquid ooze out of the yellow eyes, now dull and bloodshot, and begin to rain down upon my face. They are warm, then cold and solid. The quavery, rusty voice floats down to me, "You. Are. The. New. One. Now."

With a strength I didn't know I had, I force myself up. I beat away the mask face and push aside the shimmering air of the room through which my scream is still echoing. Chairs and side tables fall as I crash past them. Magazines fly through the air and crash against the walls.

"Hey, Fink-face! What are you doing out there? Demolition derby?" I have no voice to answer Lucas.

I reach the phone in the hall just outside the bathroom door. I grab the receiver. I dial 911. I wait through a century of rings. Finally someone answers. "Do you wish police, ambulance, or fire?"

My voice is choked with sobs. "Police, oh, police. Please hurry."

Click. The line goes dead. Cold gentle fingers touch the back of my neck. I drop the receiver, which swings like a pendulum, banging against the wall, a dull hollow sound. I fall to the ground like a stone, like a piece of raw meat, and bury my face in my hands. My hands smell like skunk cabbage, no, like swamp water, no, like the bacon that somebody forgot in the back of the fridge. My face is smooth and cold and becoming more solid every second. My hair begins to move on my scalp. They have me. I am becoming one of them. I feel my brain hardening inside my head. I hold on to one thought. My dear twin. My brother. My boon companion. Fellow traveler on the road of life. Oh, God, don't let them take Lucas.

I try to picture the bathroom window. Oh, please, let him be skinny enough to get through it. My mouth is becoming rigid. I use up my last human words. "Lucas, break the window. Get out. For pity's sake don't come out here."

Then silence. The only sound is the telephone receiver thudding against the wall.

"Amy? You're just kidding, aren't you? That was pretty good. You know, if you weren't so funny looking, you could probably become an actress."

Silence.

Lucas's voice shrinks. "Amy? Amy, come on. Quit it."

Beep, beep, beep. The telephone's humanoid voice rings out in the silent hall.

"Please hang up and try your call again. If you need assistance, dial your operator. Please hang up now. Beep, beep, beep."

The bathroom door opens slowly. I'm curled up behind it. I hold my breath. Two steps, that's all I need. Two measly steps.

"Amy?"

Two steps it is. I grab the door, swing around it, jump into the bathroom, and turn the lock.

Success! Triumph! Oh, happiness, oh, joy! I shake my own hand.

I slurp some cold water from the tap. My throat hurts a bit from that final scream. But it was worth it. It was one of the better screams of my career. There's something to be said for really scaring yourself.

R. L. Tankard is sitting on the back of the toilet. I open him up. R. L. Tankard is such a good writer that he can make you forget all about what's going on around you. He can make you forget, for example, a flipped-out twin brother using inappropriate language on the other side of the bathroom door. Listen. He's already repeating himself. Really, his repertoire of invective is pathetically inadequate. He should do more reading to increase his word power.

I settle down on the bath mat and find my page. So—what *was* in that baby's room?

CATCH

"It's a rite of passage," said my aunt Darlene.

We were sitting in an ice-cream parlor celebrating the fact that I had just passed my driving test.

Darlene raised her Coke float. "Welcome to the adult world. May all your parallel parks be perfect."

I held up a spoonful of hot fudge sundae. "To a good teacher." Darlene had been a good teacher, patient and funny. She had taken over my driving instruction from Dad, who got so nervous with me at the wheel that he burped all the time.

"She'll talk your ear off," Dad warned.

She did, a continuous commentary insulting the behavior of other drivers. It made my nervousness dissolve. I'll take that over burping anytime.

"We just don't have enough rituals for these occasions," said Darlene. "We really need something in this culture—a chant or a dance or some libation to the goddess of the road."

"Ice cream is just fine," I said.

"These passages in our lives are what connect us to the great cycles of existence . . ."

French vanilla, black raspberry, tropical fruit swirl. Sometimes I don't pay total attention to Darlene. I glanced above the list of flavors to the clock on the wall.

"Hey, Darlene. It's 5:20. We have to go. I have orchestra tonight."

Darlene slurped the last of her drink and then returned the glass to the counter. She stopped to compliment the waitress on her product and her excellent service.

I jiggled on the balls of my feet. Darlene is a great person with no grip on time.

Just as we were heading out the door, an old man spoke to Darlene. He had gray hair and a dirty khaki raincoat and he was sitting alone.

Darlene stopped. "What's that? I didn't catch what you said."

The man looked up and said, in a cracking voice, "My little king is gone."

Oh, no. I glanced back at the clock. It was really time to go. I tried to catch Darlene's eye but she was pulling up a chair to sit next to the old man.

"Do you know where he is?"

Dar*lene*, he's one of those mumblers. Come *on*.

The old man shook his head. "He just went away."

"Okay. When did you see him last?"

Why was she having this nutso conversation?

"At the park. I took off his leash and he chased a squirrel."

"So King is your dog?"

The old man nodded and turned away.

Darlene stood up and pushed her chair into the table with a clang. "Come on then, we'll look for him."

"Darlene," I half whispered, "my rehearsal. I have to be leaving from home in twenty minutes."

"Rita, this man has lost his dog. We have priorities here."

The old man didn't walk very well so Darlene put him in the front seat of the car and we set off into rush-hour traffic. Up streets and down alleys. Darlene talked a mile a minute and the old man said nothing. I cranked open the backseat window to let out the musty, sharp, old-man smell.

Half an hour and several illegal left-hand turns later we found the dog—a lanky, hairy off-white mutt nosing in a garbage can. The old man barely waited for the car to stop before he was out the door. Darlene watched him hugging the dog for a few seconds and then we drove away.

By the time we escaped from the snarl of traffic and were on the road home, we were nearly an hour late and everything was making me furious. I was furious at the stupid ugly dog for running away. I was furious at the smelly old man, who didn't even say thank you. I was furious at Darlene for getting involved. I sat in the corner of the backseat and chewed on my fury. I *hate* being late.

Mom and Dad were out when we got back home. Darlene came in with me and asked if it would help if she fixed me some supper.

"Supper! I don't even have time to get there now. I've missed the bus and they only run every forty-five minutes. I *can't* miss this rehearsal. It's the last one before the Christmas concert."

"Oh, honey, I would drive you but I've got my realignment class tonight."

Darlene explained her realignment class to me once. They realign something, their spines or the universe.

"Hang on! I've got it. I'll get a ride with someone and you can borrow my car."

"Alone?"

"Sure, you've got a license. Why not?"

I glanced at the clock. There was no time to make this decision. I took a deep breath.

"Sure. Thanks."

I grabbed my oboe and music and ran out to the car. It felt very big and lonely as I slid inside. I adjusted the seat and both mirrors. I figured out the headlights and where the high beams were, in case a dark country road should suddenly appear between my house and the art center. I put my hands at ten o'clock and two o'clock and set off. I drove just under the speed limit and cars kept coming up close behind and swerving around in a snarly way. I tried one of Darlene's lines. "Don't waste those valuable microseconds, buddy." It wasn't that helpful. At night, when you can't see the drivers, cars seem alive, like wild animals in the jungle.

When I arrived at the arts center, there was no time to search for parking on the street, so I pulled into the underground lot. It was very full. Must have been some concert on. Four minutes. I corkscrewed down and down and the car clock seemed to speed up. Finally I found a space. It took me three tries to back the car between a van and a pillar. I grabbed my oboe case and squeezed out the door sideways, grateful that I didn't play the cello. I ran through the rows of cars to the elevator, caught it just as the door was closing, slid up to the music school, sprinted to the rehearsal room, and plunked down in my seat three minutes late.

I slid out of my jacket and started to put together my oboe. My nose began to drip. As I leaned forward to get a Kleenex from my jacket pocket, I knocked the music stand. It started to tip and Yvette, my stand partner, caught it and set it back in place, very precisely. She gave me a little pitying smile. She looked cool and perfect as usual. Yvette probably has a special drip-free nose to go with her zit-free complexion. I wanted to kick her.

Behind me, Claude, who plays English horn, was sucking his reed very enthusiastically. It was a loud, wet slurpy sound. I wanted to kick him, too.

Mr. Farland stepped up to the podium and raised his eyebrows. "Quite settled, Rita? Then let's begin. Now that we've got all the double reeds here, why don't we start with the Bach."

Mr. Farland had done an arrangement for oboes, English horns, and bassoons from Bach's "Art of the Fugue." Before we had played it for the first time, he had given us a long lecture, all about counterpoint and mirror fugues and canons. I understood the first part okay, how fugues are like rounds or catches, like "Row, Row, Row Your Boat." "You'll be chasing each other," said Mr. Farland. But then his explanation got very complicated and the whole thing sounded like mathematical snoresville to me. Snoresville until we played it, that is. Even that first time, with its squeaks and blats and total breakdown halfway through, I knew I was going to love being inside this music.

We had practiced a lot and I thought it was ready to go. But something happened that night. Mr. Farland counted us in and the oboes started. We sounded plain and small. Then the English horns took over the melody and we hovered above them. But the best moment came when the bassoons entered below us all. It was like being lifted up by a giant warm wind; our chairs levitated off the floor.

All my leftover fury and the tension of the jungle drive dissolved, and I felt as though my oboe were a part of my body, its sound my voice. And it wasn't just me. I heard parts of the melody above and below me, before and after me, and I felt the gentle tug of all the lines of sound, a web.

Yvette with her attitude, gross Claude, grumpy me—even sarcastic Mr. Farland and some composer who's been dead for two hundred and fifty years—we were all connected.

When we finished, Jamal, the first bassoonist, punched the air with his fist. "Yes!" And we all laughed. I laughed because I had to let the bigness out.

"That was terrific," said Mr. Farland. "You really reminded us that you are *WIND* instruments. Whatever you did tonight, bottle it for the concert."

The rest of the rehearsal was fine. The Bach was playing inside me when we finished and I headed back to the car. But when I got off the elevator, Bach vanished as I stared at the two opposite glass doors leading out into the lot and realized I had no idea where the car was. I closed my eyes and tried to remember which way I had come. It was no use. It had vanished in the panic of my arrival.

I took a chance on the left door. How many rows of cars had I run by? And from which direction? The parking lot was very quiet, except for that big-building hum. It was humming in the key of D. Many of the cars were gone. Spaces appeared like missing teeth. I held my music case a bit tighter and decided on a methodical approach. I would walk down each row.

Minutes later I heard the first squeal, a perfect minor chord. Then three more squeals and a car pulled up just behind me. It slowed down.

"Hey! Want a ride to your car?"

I didn't look. "No, thank you." I kept on walking. Calmly, not speeding up.

"Aw, come on. Why don't you want a ride? We've got treats in here. Don't you want to see?"

The car kept pace with me, just behind me as I walked, and I started to get a pounding in my ears. I tried to think of the fastest way back to the elevator.

I ducked into the next row. I heard the car squeal around the corner and it came toward me as I came out from behind a pillar. This time I saw them. Three men in a black convertible.

It was another voice. "I don't think she likes us. Why don't you like us, little girl?"

"I think she's a stuck-up bitch, that's what I think. I think we need to teach her a lesson."

Oh, please let there be another noise, of another car, or of footsteps. Why didn't someone come? But there was only the hum and the voices and my heart beating in my ears.

I started to run, weaving in and out of cars. My shoes slapped on the white floor. My shoulder caught the side of a truck and I spun around. The squealing sound was continuous, an animal being slaughtered, and I couldn't tell what direction it was coming from.

And then Darlene's car appeared. I fumbled for the keys in my purse. The squealing was louder and a voice echoed through the bright shadowless light, "What is this, hide-and-seek?"

The key trembled in the lock and then I was in. I turned the key in the ignition and the engine coughed once and died. I tried to breathe and to remember Darlene's instructions. Pump the gas pedal three times.

And then the convertible was there. In front of my car. Trapping me. The three men got out and in that second I wondered if my back doors were locked. I was frozen in the seat. I couldn't turn around to look.

There was a crash as a beer bottle hit the pillar beside me. I stared at the brown liquid trickling down the whiteness. Then the car began to rock. I looked in the rearview mirror. Two men were on the trunk, jumping. I could only see legs.

Where was the third man? I twisted around in my seat. The back door on the passenger side was not locked. I started to reach for it when I heard the door click open. I pulled back sharply. Something was squeezing my lungs.

And then a beam of light came in the windshield. I saw a small gray-haired man dressed in green coveralls. He was carrying a cell phone and a big flashlight. He spoke into the phone. "Section E-3. Section E-3, police emergency."

The three men scrambled out from the back, yelling. They shoved the green man aside and jumped into their car. They squealed away.

I had to get out, outside, above ground. Pump the gas pedal three times and wait five seconds. But my right foot was dancing wildly and my leg would not obey me. I leaned into the steering wheel and sobbed. When I looked up there was nobody around. I took a deep breath and made myself remember how to drive.

I circled my way up to the pay booth, telling myself out loud how to do it. When I got there the gate was smashed. There was a police car with a flashing red light and two dogs in the back. A policewoman started to ask me questions, but when she saw how much I was shaking, she went and got a blanket to put around me.

"I'm just glad that security guard turned up," I said.

"Hold it," said the parking lot guy. "We don't have security guards."

"I guess it was just a helpful citizen," said the policewoman.

They phoned home and Mom and Dad came to get me.

I stayed home from school the next day. Darlene came over and gave me soup and a foot massage. She made me tell the story quite a few times. Then she made me go driving with her even though I had decided to shred my license and stick to buses for the rest of my life.

The concert was the next week. As we fell silent after tuning up and the house lights went down, I noticed three latecomers hurrying into the second row. It was Mom, Dad, and Darlene. They had come together because Darlene's car was in the shop getting the dents bashed out. Darlene was wearing an off-the-shoulder red sequined dress. She gave me a finger wave. I smiled back. I'll bet she had made them late. I'll bet Dad was burping.

The concert went well. The Bach, which we played just before the intermission, was fine. All the notes were right and we didn't drag and nobody squeaked. But our chairs stayed on the floor. Whatever it was that night, it didn't make it into the bottles.

After the concert there was hot apple juice and gingerbread in the lobby. Mom got all teary the way she does. Dad got cornered by a whiny woman complaining about the Christmas carol medley. Why had we played all those carols nobody had heard of? What happened to "Silent Night"? I turned my back and kept a low profile. Darlene joined them so I kept on eavesdropping. Darlene is more than a match for any whiner.

"Don't you think it is significant that it is a proven scientific fact that music rearranges our mental syntax, making us much more open to the positive forces of the universe? I find that especially important as we approach the shortest day of the year. I mean, especially if you're phototropic like I am . . ."

I snuck a peek. The whiner was looking hunted and edging away.

As we prepared to leave, Darlene said, "Philip, why don't you just go get the car and pick us up at the front door." She flexed one high-heeled foot. "My shoes hurt." Dad rolled his eyes but he went. Mom kept him company.

I squeezed Darlene's skinny arm. Sometimes she knows things that other people don't, like how a person could really not want to go into the underground parking garage, even with three other people.

We went outside and Darlene lit a cigarette. "I've been thinking about something. You know the security guard that helped you that night? What did he look like?"

"Darlene, I've told you a bunch of times. Short, sort of strong-looking, gray hair, wrinkled forehead, and dressed in one of those jumpsuit things that mechanics wear, green."

Darlene nodded. "Yeah, that would be the old guy from the ice-cream place."

"What?"

"You know, the one who lost his dog. Did you recognize him?"

"No, but . . . I don't remember what the dog man looked like, and the man in the parking lot, I hardly looked at him. First there was the bright light and then he just disappeared."

Darlene nodded. "Yes, he did what he came to do."

"But that would be an incredible coincidence. I mean, why would he be there in the parking lot at that moment?"

"Oh, honey, he just knew he had to be there to take care of you. He's obviously one of the others, not one of us. But we're all connected."

I stared at Darlene as she took a long drag on her cigarette. "One of the others." I hadn't heard about "the others." I suspected I was going to, probably right after the next puff. It would only take one question. The ancient power of ritual, the realignment of the cosmos, the healing effects of music, the interconnection of all things on the planet—Darlene isn't one to keep the good news to herself.

The car pulled up. The passenger door swung open. I grabbed Darlene's hand and pulled her in after me.

NET

I remember when I first started reading backward. I was in the car. Dad pulled up to a stop sign. STOP. I read the letters and made the word, and then my mind did a little flip around to the back of the sign, to the silver side, and with my special X-ray vision I read it backward. POTS. Stop pots. Stop pots. I walked around the sign inside my head until Dad pulled through the inter-section. I must have been about six years old. I have been doing backward reading ever since.

Backward reading led me, after a few years, to palindromes. Tuna Nut. Evil Olive. Gnu Dung. Tarzan Raised Desi Arnaz' Rat. Now I could not only walk back and forth through words, I could stand at the still center and let the letters spin around me. "Satan, Oscillate My Metallic Sonatas." Balance on that middle *y* and the letters march away identically in both directions.

Palindromes led me to Nadia. But to tell you about Nadia I must go forward and backward. Forward from that stop sign and backward from this moment.

In September, when I left home to go to the university,

Andrew gave me his three best Pogs. He's never seen a university and I think he imagines some overgrown elementary school. Paul gave me a sweater. He went to Valu Village and found a repulsive brown V-neck thing and sewed leather patches onto the elbows. He's rented *Who's Afraid of Virginia Woolf* too many times. And Dad and Mom gave me a modem and an E-mail account. It was their way of encouraging me to write home.

I never did find the Pog-playing community, or the Richard Burton dress-alikes. But I do write home. I tell them about fractals and William Faulkner and how I'm learning to cook. I tell them how my math prof wears rubber gloves to write on the blackboard. I tell them that midterm exams are over.

But I don't tell them everything. I don't tell them, for example, that I'm dissolving. How everything here is wet. It rains day after gray dripping day. My basement apartment has one window. I need to turn on the lights even at noon. Black mildew is creeping across the bathroom ceiling. The towels never dry. And once I came home and found a slug on the side of the toilet.

On campus it's foggy. You walk along and you don't see another person and the sound of the foghorns echoes around you. *Vwooooo-woop.* And then you go to class. Two hundred students in one huge lecture hall. And a distant man in rubber gloves writes on the blackboard and moans on. *Vwoooooo-woop.* I sit in a study carrel in the library and try to write an essay on the poems of William Butler Yeats, but my brain feels as though it is trying to walk through water.

Before I left home Dad took me out to the workshop and gave me some extra money and told me that his university years were the best years of his life and that I would remember mine forever. I couldn't E-mail home and say that I didn't write my midterms, that I had stopped going to class, that any minute it was all going to crash and bury me.

That's why I was going home today, to tell them in person. Mom was all happy when I phoned last night. It was perfect. I would be there for Andrew's birthday. She would make lasagna. Best of all, Aunt Irene was driving up and I could get a ride so she would pick me up at nine o'clock sharp and don't keep her waiting because you know how she is about time.

But all that was yesterday. An age ago. In the Pleistocene era. That was before I met Nadia.

Yesterday evening, after I talked to Mom, I gathered up all my dirty laundry (read: every single item in my wardrobe) and stuffed it in a duffel bag. Then I sat down at my desk and logged onto the Net. Just to kill some time. I cruised around a bit. Friday-night losers unite. I had one of my usual scintillating Net conversations:

"Hi."

"Hi, where are you from?"

"Canada. You?"

"Florida."

"What's in Florida?"

"Half the population of Canada. ;-)"

Great. A winker. I played along with a grin: ":-) What's your name?"

"Lauren. Yours?"

What was the point of all this drivel? I felt like ending it all with a yawn, :-o , but I find it hard to be rude, even in cyberspace. I plowed on. "Aidan."

And then another voice broke in.

"Aidan! My palindromic alter ego! Where have you been all my life?"

It was signed "Nadia."

As soon as she appeared she was so real, so there. There was no chatter, no sniffing around. We were inside each other's heads right away. I had no idea that there was a person who thought about the things I thought about.

We started right away. Why is it terrifying to think of the not-being that may come after death and not terrifying to think of the not-being that most certainly existed before birth? If a person's brain were transplanted into another person's head, who would the original person be, the brain or the body? What could you do that would be so bad that you would have to kill yourself for shame? Who do you hate most from when you were a kid and what would you most like to do to them? If global warming caused Antarctica to melt, would the weight of the north polar ice cap cause the whole world to flip over, north over south? Would that be the ultimate palindromic experience? Would everyone in North America start acting like Australians? Is Ronald McDonald really a clown? Why do people alone in cars think you can't see them picking their noses?

We did a little forum-cruising together. Nadia stuck her nose in everywhere, joking or raging. We found some gourmet club exchanging veal recipes. Nadia jumped in and wrote, "Skinless: Red flesh, yellow veins, black blood, white muscles iridescent as oil. Watch me move. Eat me." She didn't add a grin. Nadia was not afraid of being rude in cyberspace. The gourmets went into an uppercase flame session at that one. But mostly we just talked to each other. Nadia knew everything I knew but more. I told her how I used to imagine myself at the center of a palindrome pointing in both directions, and I had barely typed that in when she replied, "Yes, at the hinge. Everything ahead of me is already behind me but it looks completely different and has a different meaning."

Talking to her was like talking to myself, but not to the self I knew. With her I was a bigger, nondissolving self, and nothing was poised to crash on my head.

Time went away. Sometime in the middle of the night it stopped raining. And then minutes later the room lightened slightly and I glanced at my watch. It was eight o'clock. We had been talking for twelve hours. From some distant country I remembered Aunt Irene. I would have to get ready to go. I explained it to Nadia, for the first time talking about ordinary things.

And for the first time there was no reply. I felt a moment of panic. "Are you there? Are you there?"

She replied. "Where are you going? When?"

I gave her the details.

"Don't go."

What was this? Don't go. Why did it matter where I was? "We can talk again when I get there. It's about a ten-hour drive. I'll talk to you at seven, eight at the latest."

There was no reply. "Nadia, come back." I stared at the screen, paralyzed.

Then I got up and threw myself into the shower. The hot water ran out after a few seconds. They were running the dishwasher upstairs. I rinsed off in cold and my thoughts froze. My bath towel smelled like cheese, and I stuffed it in the duffel bag. I put on the same clothes I had taken off. I drank some milk out of the carton. I dribbled onto my shirt. The screen was still blank.

At two minutes to nine Aunt Irene rapped at my door. On the second rap a message appeared on the screen.

"Just a minute!"

It was short. "Aidan. I need to see you. Harry's Billiards. Ten o'clock this morning. Nadia."

"Aidan, are you ready?"

I opened the door and Irene came in and gave me a hug. "Is this all you have?" She pointed to the duffel bag.

"Yeah. Just a minute." I needed to think. I went into the bathroom and sat on the toilet. She lived here. What were the chances of this? :-D :-D :-D. Last night it didn't matter. Planet Earth was a close enough address. But now that I knew she was in this very city there was no choice. I had to see her.

"Aidan, I'm taking your bag out to the car. I'll meet you there."

"Irene? Hang on." She was gone.

I emerged from the bathroom and sat down to type an answer. "Yes, I'll come, but where is Harry's and how will I know you?"

No answer. I waited.

I typed again. "Okay. I'll find it. I'll know you."

Irene stuck her head back in the door and tapped her watch. "Aidan, it's after nine. We have a schedule here."

I stood up. "I can't go, Irene. I'm really sorry. I'll phone Mom and explain but I just can't. Something has come up."

Irene gave me a hard look. "Are you in trouble, Aidan?"

"No, no. I'm fine. Really. I'm sorry I made you late."

"Okay, but look, if anything *is* wrong, don't just slog through it by yourself, okay? I know what you're like. We'll call tonight."

I went out to the car and retrieved my bag. Then I went back inside and panicked.

Where was Harry's Billiards? Where was the phone book? It was propping up one end of the bookcase. I pulled it out and stuck in *The Collected Poems of W. B. Yeats.* I got temporary dyslexia and couldn't remember the alphabet. I found the address and phoned the transit information line. They put me on hold. I had to listen to "Jambalaya" about seven million times.

I was just about to leave when I noticed the crusty dried milk on my shirt. It was my last clean thing. Except . . . I grabbed a paring knife and sawed the patches off my Richard Burton sweater. I would just have to keep my jacket zipped up, at least for the first impression.

Harry's was clear across town and I had to transfer twice. I got there at 10:10. I looked around with a "here-I-am" look. Nobody looked back. I drank coffee. And I thought every thought. She was there at ten but she left. I was in the wrong Harry's. She had been in a terrible accident. I thought every thought twice. Every time a woman came in the door I went hollow. But nobody was looking for anybody. I ordered a sandwich. I didn't eat it. I got a buzzing in my head and the click of the billiard balls seemed amplified. I started to look at old women and children and men, and to wonder if they were her.

She didn't show. At one o'clock I left. I could not face a bus crowded with people who were not Nadia. So I walked. After about a block it hit me why she hadn't come. It was because she didn't exist. It had all been a complicated trick to make a fool of me. Some cretinous fart-faced hacker, some turd-brain. With each step I became angrier. What, did this pervert have no life or what? I kicked the wet leaves on the sidewalk as though they were somebody's face. There were lots of faces. Bus drivers who pull away just as you reach the stop and leave you standing in the rain and you miss your first class, but who cares anyway. That cool guy with the Miata who doesn't come out to turn off his stupid car alarm at three in the morning. Cheap landlords who won't turn up the heat. Professors who give you a *C* on a paper and don't even say what you did wrong. People in Sociology 100 who look at you like you're a worm on the make when you say something to them but really you just wanted to talk.

I stepped on them all, along main streets and side streets and alleys and across soggy playing fields. "Bog dirt up a sidetrack carted is a putrid gob." Sometime in the night Nadia and I had invented this palindrome. I said it over and over again, silently, to the rhythm of my avenging feet. I walked for two hours.

When I got home I went straight to the computer. I punched in her address. "Incorrect address." Right. I didn't try again.

I turned on the TV while I took off my shoes and sodden socks. I flipped through the channels. Dancing breakfast cereal, a lion yawning, Aunt Irene, talking heads . . . What? I flipped back a channel. A varnished-hair announcer was holding a microphone in front of Aunt Irene. They were standing against the backdrop of a huge muddy boulder. A flashing light lit the boulder at intervals.

". . . so, as I drove around the curve I heard a roar. And then a whole piece of the mountain just fell away. Rocks, trees. I hit the brakes and the next thing I knew the car was covered in mud. When I got out to look, the road in front of me had just disappeared."

"I guess you're glad you didn't hit this stretch of road a couple of minutes earlier?"

Aunt Irene's voice started to quiver. "Oh, yes."

Varnish-head took back his mike and stared out at us in that sincere announcer way. "Police on the scene say that it is a near miracle that there were no fatalities, on such a crowded holiday weekend."

We returned to the newsroom. "That was a report from this

morning's spectacular landslide on the mountain highway. Meanwhile, road crews are on the scene, but the highway will be closed until further notice. With a backgrounder on this notoriously dangerous road we have reporter Sue Hackett. Sue, were the heavy rains of the last few weeks a factor . . ."

The phone rang.

"Aidan?"

It was Mom. I had completely forgotten to phone and tell her that I wasn't coming home. I couldn't fit a word in.

"Oh, thank goodness. We just turned on the news. Mark! Mark, it's okay, he's home. We just got back from Andrew's soccer game and then we had that garage sale thing at the school. Then we were watching the news. And it was the first we heard. How are you? And how's Irene? She must be feeling very shaken up. What do you mean, you weren't with her? Andrew, just a minute. Oh, I just hate that highway."

"Were you nearly dead?"

"Andrew, get off the phone. You can talk to Aidan in a minute."

It took quite a lot of sorting out. Especially because everyone got on the phone at once. Mom talked about a guardian angel and then she cried. Dad got all gruff and said that maybe this would make them stop logging the watershed. Paul made eerie woo-woo sounds. Andrew said that if I wasn't dead the least I could do was get interviewed on TV. Somehow in the confusion nobody asked me why I hadn't been coming home after all.

After I hung up I went to sit at the computer, in its pool of blue underwater light. I stared at the screen, at my own reflection. I thought about leaving on time and Irene's little green Honda crushed under that boulder, or pushed off the side of the mountain. With both of us in it.

Delete. Save. What would it be like to be deleted, gone? I let myself feel the hollowness of being nowhere.

Nowhere. No where. Now here. Saved. Alive.

"I need to see you." That was her last message. I typed it backward. "Uoy ees ot deen I." Forward or backward, it didn't mean anything. Except it meant that she did exist. Or at least she did last night. Then. There.

Suddenly the room began a slow spin. I held on to the edge of the table. Maybe Antarctica was melting. I looked at my gripping hands. They didn't seem to have much to do with me—hands, computer, windowsill, coffee cup. A collection of random floating objects, not on or with or beside. Thirty-some hours without sleep and the world loses its prepositions, thirty-some hours without sleep and the glue goes out of things.

"Turning and turning . . . the center cannot hold." It was the Yeats poem, the poem I had spent hours staring at. It made some new sense. I saw a palindrome beginning to spin so fast that the safe unmoving center rips apart and the whole thing flies out into the darkness. I rubbed my eyes and typed a note onto the screen. "Yeats, palindromes, prepositions, glue." Tomorrow I would write that essay.

I looked at the window, to my ghost-faced reflection. My eyes looking at my eyes looking at my eyes. A closed loop. I put the computer to sleep. The light faded and my face disappeared. I looked out into the dim beyond.

SISTERS

Mrs. Fenner's funeral was on the first day of spring. It was windy. The sky was a map of islands, gray and white, on a sea of washed-out blue. The islands dissolved and merged, continental drift in fast forward.

At the cemetery I stared hard at the clouds. I looked up to keep from looking at the ground, into the ground. Most of the words the minister said were cloud-words. *Mercy, hope, peace*—thin words whipped away by the wind. And a few earth-words. *Ashes, blood, bread, grass.* The grass at the cemetary was still yellow-dry from winter. The grave was a bright green box, lined with AstroTurf. Mrs. Fenner was the first person I knew who died. I think.

Afterward I went home with Miss Poole and helped pass out sandwiches. The guests were the minister, Mrs. Fenner's businessman son, Robert, who flew in from Toronto, and some friends who live in Mrs. Fenner and Miss Poole's building. The sandwiches were ham or egg salad. Then there were butter tarts and ginger cookies. Mrs. Sutherland from 604 brought a pan of fudge squares. There was tea and sherry. Robert Fenner poured out the sherry from a decanter shaped like a Scotsman with bow legs and a bright yellow-and-red kilt. His tartan tam was the stopper. Mrs. Fenner had made the decanter when she took up ceramics. She had also made frogs to hold hand soap and ceramic potatoes to hold sour cream. People talked a lot about all the things she had made. The things she had left behind. Then they all went away.

I should explain about Mrs. Fenner and Miss Poole. They are my foster grandmothers. I got them the year my sister, Sophie, ran away the first time. Mom and Dad thought I should have foster grandparents because my real ones live in Florida and France. They thought we needed more people in our family.

The foster-grandparent organizers sent us to meet three regular grandfather/grandmother pairs. One pair had a dog who liked me. One had a cottage in the mountains. "We could take you there in the summer if you'd like that, Charlotte."

One had a lot of computer games. But I didn't want any of them to be my grandparents. When Mom asked me why I said, "They look at me too hard." I was only nine. I didn't know how to say that they had a kind of hungry look, that they made me feel like a rent-a-kid.

And then we met Mrs. Fenner and Miss Poole, two sisters. The first time we visited them, we all sat at the kitchen table with old magazines, scissors, glue, and cardboard ice-cream buckets. Mrs. Fenner was into decoupage that year. The sisters talked to each other and to Mom. The words floated over my head as I cut and pasted. "I think young Charlotte has remarkable color sense," Miss Poole said to Mrs. Fenner. Their fat cat Ditto jumped onto the table and overturned the glue. Miss Poole held him close to her face and growled at him. Mrs. Fenner showed me how to pick up tiny bits of paper by licking the end of my finger. We had tea and the afternoon disappeared. On the way home, hugging my decorated wastepaper basket, I told Mom that Mrs. Fenner and Miss Poole were my choice.

From then on I went over to their apartment lots of days after school. Sometimes the grans took me out. Fridays we went to early-bird bingo at the Catholic hall. Mrs. Fenner played eight cards at once and was calm even when she won. Miss Poole sat on the edge of her chair, talked to the numbers on her card, and made mistakes. The lady who gave out the bingo prizes was young and pretty, with red hair like Sophie. Sometimes I used to pretend she *was* Sophie and that one day she would peer down from the stage through the smoke and recognize me, her little sister.

"Charlotte! Is that you?" Then she would come home with us for good, bringing all the bingo prizes. We would get on the bus carrying lamps and cookware sets and embroidered pillowcases and we would all laugh. I had strange ideas when I was nine and ten.

We stopped going to bingo when Mrs. Fenner's leg got bad. Mostly we just stayed in. I would sit at the kitchen table and make sand-cast candles or macramé belts and listen to them talk. The grans came from a village in England and they remembered all the people there. I got to know them, too. Addie's Harold, who was a "right terror" until they gave him a ferret to care for. "Mind you, it did take one aback when that little ferret face would peek out of his shirt." Stanley, who ran in the Empire Games. "It was a miracle. To think of him being that poor weak baby. Ada had to carry him around on a pillow with his little legs dangling over." And Jeannie, who went off to London to become a dancer. "Aunt Effie went to see her, a surprise like, and they put her at a table right near the front and when Jeannie came out, she didn't have a stitch on, just a few of them feathers. Well, Eff just didn't know where to look. Mind, she never told Jean's mum, it would have killed her."

When I got older Mom thought I went to visit the grans because I was being good. "It's so kind of you to go and see them," she said.

Kind had nothing to do with it. I went there to escape the silence that was our house. I went there for the words. And for the people.

I went there for Addie's Harold and Stanley and feathered Jeannie. I went there for mild Alf Minkin, who wouldn't say boo to a goose and then one day upped and pelted the grocer's van with two dozen eggs. For beautiful Emily, known as Pigeon, who fell in love five times in one year and threw herself down the well for the sixth. For Jack, who revealed his true nature that night in the badger blind and had to emigrate. For Alice, the grans' older sister, who went a bit wild and ran off when she was a teenager. "And she landed on her feet, didn't she, Ida? I expect young Sophie will be just the same." The grans talked about Sophie, even though they had never met her. I couldn't talk about her. Her name stuck in my throat.

But I didn't have to talk at the grans'. It was a place for listening. Best of all was listening to Miss Poole's stories of dead people. Car-accident victims who haunt certain highways, dead husbands who leave messages in the melting snow, indelible stains—"And they scrubbed and scrubbed but the kitchen floor would never come clean. Then one day they found an old scrapbook in the attic, filled with yellowing newspaper clippings. And there was the story, the grizzly murder that had taken place years before, in that very house, in that very kitchen."

"Hush up, Ida, you're just flapping your tongue," Mrs. Fenner would sometimes say when she remembered that I was a child and might be scared. Miss Poole never thought of that. I knew that she didn't think of me as a child. Just the way she didn't think of Ditto as a cat. She just talked. To people, animals, the radio, the kettle, and the bunions on her feet. Anyway, I wasn't scared. Those were my favorite stories. I continued to visit the grans because their apartment was full of people. They crowded onto the sofa, hung around the doorways, leaned against the fridge, sat on the floor hugging their knees to fit. There were babies on the bed with the coats, and little kids hiding under the table. People jostling, elbowing, stepping on the cat by mistake, and talking, talking, talking. Noisy ghosts.

We have a ghost in our house, too. A silent ghost. The ghost of Sophie, who came home once, twice, and never again, who last phoned five years ago. She floats around the house like a piece of empty air. They used to talk about her. They used to argue. Once I heard Dad yelling, "She's gone, Trish. Accept it." But now the Sophie ghost has silenced even my parents, who never mention her.

Last Christmas, when I was helping Dad unpack the tree ornaments, he pulled out Sophie's stocking. He stared at it for a minute. I wanted to say something, something like, "I expect she landed on her feet." But the words couldn't push through the silence. Dad just packed the stocking back into the box and went outside to put up the lights. I think he forgot I was there. Sophie settles like fog on Christmas and birthdays and memories.

No, I'm not a citizen-of-the-week teenager visiting the elderly. I go to the grans to keep from dissolving into a ghost myself.

* * *

After everyone left I stayed to help Miss Poole tidy up. We took a few dirty dishes into the kitchen and then Miss Poole said, "Leave this for a minute. Come sit down." I was surprised. Miss Poole likes to get jobs over and done with. And sitting is not her style. She is always jumping up to make tea or adjust the radio or water the African violets.

She perched on the edge of her chair. Ditto did a figure-of-eight around her feet. I glanced sideways quickly at Mrs. Fenner's armchair, the big one, hoping to catch someone in it. Mrs. Fenner or someone else. It was empty.

Miss Poole beat a little drumroll on her knees, reached into a patchwork pocket that hung over the arm of the chair, and pulled out an envelope.

"Muriel left me a letter. I haven't told anyone about it yet, except Ditto. Didn't fancy discussing it with Robert, somehow. He's not much of a one for talk about the old days."

There was a large waiting feeling in the air.

"She wasn't my sister."

What?

"She was my aunt."

"Your aunt?" I couldn't figure it out. I've never been good at all that relative stuff, cousins once removed and all that.

Miss Poole gave the letter a sharp slap with the back of her hand.

"It's all there. Alice was my mother."

Alice. The other sister. Alice who was no better than she should be. Twice-divorced Alice who finally took off for America with a weedy little man who told her he was rich and, surprise of surprises, was. Alice who lived out her final days, "eaten up with the cancer she was," in New Mexico on a hacienda or some such thing.

"You mean Alice who ran away?"

"The very one. Old toffee-nosed Alice." Miss Poole snorted. "She had me when she was fifteen. So the whole family upped and moved and when they got to the next place, they just let on I was the new baby in the family. Mum took me on, just like she took on Uncle Harry when he started having his turns. And then Muriel and Mr. Fenner took me on when they came here to Canada. Isn't that a turn-up for the books?"

I was still having trouble with the generations. "So who was your mom?"

"Alice."

"No, I mean the one you call Mum."

"Well, she was really my grandmother. Look, come here." Miss Poole scribbled a diagram on the envelope. "Here's Mum. Two little lines down, that's Muriel and Alice, and from Alice one little line down to me."

"They never told you this?"

"It was the shame of it. With Dad being a church warden and all. And perhaps they thought it would give me a bad feeling about myself. One of those traumas they discuss on those television talk shows."

"And you never knew till now?"

Miss Poole leaned back in her chair a little and Ditto jumped into her lap. "Is there another cup in that pot?"

I poured out some thick-looking tea and handed it to her. "It's not very hot."

"But nice and strong. Just the way I like it." Miss Poole stared out the window for a minute. "The thing of it is, I did know. Not to say anything. And not the real truth. But I knew that I didn't match. All those Pooles. They were so big and calm. They kind of just set where you put them. But I was little and I couldn't sit still."

"Hyperactive?"

"Is that what they call it now? They wouldn't have me in school. I wouldn't stay at the desk. And meals. Dad couldn't stand the fidgeting. Mostly I ate my dinner sitting on the stairs. The other thing was I was the wrong color. Too brown. All those pink blond people. Neighbors would comment on it and Mum used to say, 'That Ida, she does take the sun so.' Come to think of it now, I suppose I took after my father. Whoever he was when he was at home."

Miss Poole took a gulp of tea and looked at the letter again.

"I'm not denying that it is a bit of a shock, though. Perhaps not quite in the way that Muriel expected. The biggest thing is . . ." Miss Poole looked at me and grinned. "You'll be thinking I'm a dafty."

"No, I won't. What?"

"I always thought I was a fairy."

"What, with wings?"

"No, not that kind. A changeling. You don't know about them? You with all your algebra and computers." Miss Poole leaned over and punched me on the arm. "Fairies want human children so they steal them away and leave their own babies, changelings, in their place. It made perfect sense to me. Changelings are dark. I was dark. Changelings cry a lot. Mum told me what a difficult baby I had been, crying and grizzling and never sleeping through the night. I just tucked those things away in my head."

I thought of a little girl sitting on the stairs eating her dinner and thinking she was some weird kind of fairy. It made me want to hug Miss Poole. But she's not a hugger.

"Did you think you were a fairy even when you grew up?"

"Well I did and I didn't. Things got very busy when we emigrated to Canada, what with keeping the house going and taking care of Robert while Muriel and Mr. Fenner went out to work. I didn't think about it all that much, to tell you the truth. But I had it all tucked away. And sometimes . . . like, one time we had this boarder. We were having a hard time making ends meet and we took in boarders. And there was this one called Merv Butt and he was a great one for making beer. He tried to make beer out of everything. He even boiled down our Christmas tree that year to try to make spruce beer. And here I was, a great grown-up girl, as old as you, and I still thought that that was proof."

"Proof? I don't get it."

"Because of trying to fool the changeling. Sometimes people could get their own babies back by tricking the changeling into revealing herself. They would act silly to try to get the changeling to speak. Like in one story the people boil water in an eggshell and the changeling baby sits up in the cradle and says, 'I never in all my life saw water boiled in an eggshell.' And then the changeling has to leave. So I thought that making beer out of a Christmas tree was the same thing. I was very careful never to act surprised."

"It sounds a bit lonely."

Miss Poole shook her head. "It wasn't that way. It made me feel strong. Magic, immortal, all that good fairy stuff. And it explained things. Anyway, people do that all the time. Make themselves up. I mean, look at those movie stars. They take them out to Hollywood and glam them up and give them new names and make them famous. But I did it all by myself."

Miss Poole looked over at Mrs. Fenner's chair. "She was very good to me, was Muriel. Very good."

She absently pulled Ditto's ears. He broke into a loud rasping purr. "Who's my favorite boy?"

Then she suddenly sat forward, dumping Ditto. "Did we ever tell you about the time Muriel bought that goat at the fall fair? Well, you know how Muriel was not what you'd call a small woman? It seems this goat . . ."

The phone rang. "Bother, that will be Olivia. I'll get it in the bedroom." Olivia was Robert's wife. According to the grans, if you put your drink next to her, it would stay cold all evening.

I picked up some dirty dishes, took them into the kitchen, and piled them by the sink. I looked out the window. The clouds parted and the sun angled into the room, throwing a shadow of the frog soap dish onto the fridge. I sent my mind out to the cemetery where Mrs. Fenner was. The trees and the tombstones would be making long shadows. I held up two fingers and gave the frog antennae. Ditto leaned against my leg and I thought about the different kinds of gone. I wondered about Mrs. Fenner and the goat. I thought about remembering, naming, and telling.

Miss Poole bustled into the kitchen and made a horrible face. "She wants me to come and visit for Christmas. Very kind and all but I can't imagine anything more dismal. I'm thinking that I had better make some plans to protect myself. There's a seniors' bus trip to Edmonton before Christmas. The West Edmonton Mall, now that's something I'd like to see before I turn up my toes."

I held my hands in the sunlight and made a butterfly flutter across the fridge.

Miss Poole smiled. "That's lovely."

My sister. I wanted to say her name, to have it exist in the room, in the light and the shadows.

"Sophie taught me. She was really good at shadows because she was sort of double-jointed. She could bend her thumbs right back and gross people out."

"Oh, I know the feeling. There was a boy in the village, the youngest Crank boy, Sid. He could practically turn himself inside out. Made you sick to look at him, but you *did* look, all the same."

I suddenly remembered Sophie and me in a tent at night. I was holding the flashlight and Sophie was making huge looming shadows on the canvas walls. The terror was delicious.

I stuck my fingers out at odd angles and created another shadow. "Do you know what that is?"

"Haven't a clue."

"It's Blob Dog, Guardian of the Underworld. He was one of Sophie's best ones. The other good one was Angel Lips, High School Queen."

Miss Poole grinned. "That Sophie sounds a right caution."

A right caution. I wasn't really sure what it meant, but it had a Sophie feeling about it. Did I ever tell you about my sister? She was a *right caution*.

Miss Poole picked up a pink rosebud teacup. It was smeared with chocolate where the fudge square had melted against it. "That always happens when you have chocolate things at a tea. Seems like such a waste. I'll tell you a secret. After Muriel got beyond helping in the kitchen, I invented my own method of cleanup, very sensible it is, too."

Miss Poole held the cup up to her mouth, stuck out her tongue, and licked it clean. She handed me a cup. "Try it. This is likely the way fairies wash up."

My cup was forest green with a thin gold band. The chocolate was rich and the china was cool and both were smooth, smooth under smooth. We licked the cups clean like a pair of cats, and from the living room came a quiet hum of stories, cloud-words and earth-words, the voices of the not-gone.

FIX

I think my father had his vasectomy one kid too soon. First they had Daniel, then they had me. Then, having achieved gender balance and zero population growth, they stopped having babies. Mom refers to this decision as "when we got you father fixed." But ever since the fixing they've been picking up spare kids. First there was Tiffany, whose mother had to go away for a week of computer training and was afraid Tiffany's father would kidnap her while she was gone. Then there were Laurie and Connor, whose parents had to go to a funeral in Brandon. There was the year cousin Barry lived with us for grade twelve. Not to mention Lisette the French student from Montreal and Tachi and Yuko, the two Japanese computer geniuses here on a language course. We were in one of our rare family-of-four periods when I arrived home from soccer one Saturday afternoon and found Dad sitting on the living-room floor holding a screwdriver and looking overwhelmed. He was trying to put together my old dollhouse. I figured our family was about to expand again.

"Her name is Emma," said Dad. "Family Services called and they're short of foster homes at the moment. So we're taking her for a couple of days. Temporary family problem of some sort."

"Guess what? We won our game. Four to nothing."

Dad put down his screwdriver. "Rachel! That's fabulous! That's a first this season, isn't it?"

"Yup."

"Well, congratulations." Dad stared at the dollhouse again. "Didn't this thing used to have directions?"

"When is she arriving?"

"Around suppertime. This roof doesn't seem to fit at all. Do you think there's something missing?" Dad slid his hand under Max, who was impersonating a dog-skin rug. "Max, are you sitting on a piece of the roof?"

I looked at the roofless house, painted pieces of metal. The rag rug painted on the floor, the teddy-bear wallpaper of the baby's room, the spiral stairs, flat red and yellow tulips by the front door—it was all familiar. When I was a kid I had spent hours staring those rooms into reality.

Where was the furniture? I spied a creased paper bag and emptied it out. Bright plastic table, high chair, canopy bed. A giant miniature china toilet that took up the whole bathroom. And the stuff I had made myself—spool seats, a matchbox dresser, stamp portraits, toothpaste-cap lampshades.

"Is the doll family still around?"

"Look in the box. Do you suppose I've got this backward or something?"

I dug around in the newspaper and found them. The complete family. Father with his Superman chin, mother in an apron, smiling baby, and the brown polka-dotted dog. I called them Father, Mother, Baby, and Max. I wasn't a very original kid. They looked just the same. Mother still had her purple arm from the day I decorated her.

The delicious feeling of felt-tip marker smoothing across pale cool plastic. Except it wasn't just plastic then. It was plastic plus real.

I lined the family up on the coffee table and tried to make them real again. It almost worked. But not quite. It was like some tune that you hear perfectly inside your head but when you try to hum it, it just skitters away. Sorry, I felt like saying to the doll family, fourteen is too old.

"How old is this Emma?"

"Three, I think they said." Dad jammed the roof on and bashed the metal tabs down with the screwdriver. He missed a few times. "Oh, well, we'll call that hail damage." Mom backed in the door with two bags of groceries. "The dollhouse! What a good idea." She slid the groceries to the floor and came to sit beside us.

"It looks a bit worse for wear. Oh, Keith, you've put the garage roof on the house part. No wonder it doesn't fit. Let me fix it. Have you got the pliers?"

Mom rebuilt the house, fitting the slots neatly together and smoothing down the metal tabs. "I'm really looking forward to having a preschooler around again. But you forget how much equipment it takes. I've got a car seat from the Dhaliwals and a booster seat from Mandy at work. Daniel! Dan!"

Daniel clumped up from downstairs, blinking.

Max made his "Oh, happiness, here's Daniel, the love of my life" noise, a kind of deep "ah-roo."

"Daniel, could you get the booster seat from the trunk of the car?"

Daniel sighed and clumped out the door.

"It's a temporary toxic condition," said Dad, "caused by being seventeen. No known therapy or cure." He got up and pulled Mom to her feet. "Come on. I'll make coffee." Dad's a pharmacist. He likes to make medical jokes. We try not to encourage him. Thoughts of homework were floating just above my head, like a purple smog, so I stayed nice and low and was rearranging the dolls on the table when Daniel came back.

He dumped the booster seat on the couch and noticed the dolls. "Hey! It's the nuclear family." He scooped them up. "Unchanged after all these years. There's family values for you. This strikes me as a photo opportunity."

He brought up his latest camera and lights and a tripod and we spent the rest of the afternoon photographing the dolls. Balanced on the back of the napping Max: "Nuclear Family Climbs Sleeping Dog." In the toilet: "Nuclear Family Practices Drown-Proofing." In the microwave: "Nuclear Family Nuked." Threaded with bamboo skewers through their sleeves: "Nuclear Family Kabobs."

We escaped to the darkroom while Mom and Dad were putting a cot up in the spare room. "Excellent," said Daniel as the images appeared on the paper. The harsh light that he had used cast deep shadows on the doll's faces. Their eyes were hooded, their gentle smiles suggested terrible secrets. Their stiff hands looked like claws. In the dim red light of the darkroom the dolls turned real again. We were just putting the photos in the fixing solution when the doorbell rang.

By the time we got upstairs, everyone was already arranged. The family-care worker had her hands wrapped around a mug of coffee. Mom was standing with a plate of cookies. Dad was on the couch, leaning forward and grinning with the grin of someone who has just made a little medical joke. And Emma was sitting on a chair with her legs straight out, holding a glass of juice with both hands.

She had a miniature face and a bunch of dark red curls. She was dressed in a tartan smocked dress with matching hair clips. Her white knee socks came right up to her knees and she was very clean. Click, zzzzt. I blinked and for a second I saw it all in black and white, frozen in a dim red light.

There was munching, sipping, and chatting, and through it all Emma sat without talking or squirming. I felt like I should go over and move her little arm up and down to drink. After the family worker left, Mom took Emma into the kitchen and Dad and I unpacked Emma's two suitcases. The first suitcase contained more clothes than I have in my closet. I lifted out layer after neatly folded layer of real outfits, dresses, coordinated leggings and tunic tops, jumpers with matching sweaters, a bathrobe-and-nightgown set, a jewelry box full of hair ribbons.

Even Dad, who is wardrobe-challenged, noticed. "Wow, whatever the temporary family problem is, it sure isn't financial. I'll go rustle up some more hangers."

The second suitcase was full of toys. Costume dolls, a flowered china tea set, wooden puzzles. And a whole zoo of stuffed animals—hippo, hedgehog, giraffe, kitten, cow, lamb, teddy bear. All with big eyes and curling eyelashes and happy-happy smiles. Not one thing was ripped, chipped, faded, chewed, or decapitated. I looked over at the dollhouse sitting in the corner of the room. It looked really cheesy.

At dinner Emma sat on her booster seat and ate everything she was given. She wiped her face and hands with her napkin. She didn't say anything. But she smiled and jiggled up and down a bit when Max galloped into the room.

"Goodness," said Mom, "you're an easy little thing to have around." What were we, I thought, demon babies?

"What were we," said Daniel, "monster kids from the black lagoon?"

"Not at all," said Dad, who worries about our self-esteem. "You were charming."

Mom rolled her eyes. She doesn't believe in self-esteem.

After dinner Mom gave Emma a bubble bath. Then Daniel read to her from the big pop-up nursery rhyme book she had brought with her. Passing by the door I heard "One, two, step in some poo. Three, four, step in some more" and a small giggle. Daniel doesn't stick to the authorized version.

That night, about two in the morning, I was woken up by a thumping sound. I thought it must be Max. He's not allowed in the bedrooms at night. "Beat it, Max. Get a life." The thumping continued so I got up. The sound became fainter. I put my ear to the wall, the wall between my room and Emma's. Louder.

I went next door and there she was, a little girl in a yellow-striped nightie sitting up in bed and banging her head against the wall. The night-light shone on her face and her eyes were open, looking right at me. But she didn't seem to see me, or anything else. I found myself back in the hall, as though someone had pushed me, pushing the air out of me at the same time. There must have been something frightened in my voice because all I said at Mom and Dad's door was "Mom." And she was right there, almost still asleep.

I stood in Emma's doorway while Mom took her in her arms and rocked her and talked to her. She talked about all the animals going to sleep—Max in his dog bed, birds in their nests, and hippos in mud. And gradually Emma's eyes closed and Mom tucked her in.

The next day I tried playing dollhouse with her.

"Do you think we should get Baby up from his nap now?"

"Okay."

"You do it."

Emma took the baby out of his cradle and held it, sitting motionless.

"Maybe Baby would like to go for a ride on the swing."

"Okay."

"Put him on the swing then. What do you think Maxy is doing?"

"I don't know."

"Is Mom going to the kitchen or is she going to take a bath?"

"You pick."

Nothing makes you sound more idiotic than playing with someone who's not really playing. I started to hear myself sounding like a total dweeble. I figured out why Emma's toys were so clean. She didn't actually play with them. They were items of room decor.

Grandpa came over to dinner and pretended to steal Emma's nose. She smiled a bit. "Isn't she a doll," he said.

"Yes," I wanted to answer. "Yes, that's it exactly. She's not real flesh and blood. She's like a very, very good robot, with a program inside her that tells her how to simulate human-ness. She's virtual reality."

But I didn't say it. I just passed the potatoes.

After dinner I offered to read to Emma. It seemed like a good way to get out of cleanup. We sat on the couch with the pile of books that Mom had brought home from the library. I asked Emma which one she would like and she said, "You pick." So I did. It was *Cinderella*. I tried putting my arm around Emma, to make a circle of us and the book. But she was as uncuddly as a piece of furniture. I took my arm back and we sat side by side.

After I started reading I thought maybe the words were too old for a three-year-old, what with the wicked stepsisters "inflicting vexations" on Cinderella. But Emma was quiet and attentive. She only reacted twice. The first was to a picture of the wicked stepsister, the one with the hairy wart on her chin. She had her fist clenched and was looming over ragged Cinderella, who was crouched by the fire. Emma just put her hand over the picture.

At the first picture of the fairy godmother Emma said, "Is that a fairy?"

"Yes," I said, "that's the fairy godmother. She's magic."

As the fairy godmother changed rags to a ballgown and mice to horses—bibbedy, bobbedy, boo—Emma moved her finger carefully around the outline of the plump, white-haired, wand-waving godmother.

We read the book three times that night. On the first reread I tried to skip the stepsister picture by turning over two pages at once. But Emma firmly turned back the page so that she could cover the stepsister with her hand. We read *Cinderella* about twenty times over the next few days and Emma did the same things every time, making the warty stepsister disappear and tracing the outline of the fairy godmother.

The late-night thumping continued that night and the next. I moved my bed across the room. but the noise still woke me up. I hated waking up and then imagining those empty staring eyes on the other side of the wall.

It was a complicated week. Mom and Dad juggled their shifts at work to be home with Emma. And our soccer coach, inspired by Saturday's winning game, decided to call extra after-school skills practices to "maintain the momentum."

Thursday he was a maniac. We practiced every soccer technique in the book, ending up with a whole session on heading. "Eyes *open*. Jump with both feet. Kick behind for power. *Beautiful*." Afterward he treated us to big glasses of cold fresh-squeezed orange juice and an inspirational talk. Everyone started acting goofy and laughing at, like, nothing.

When it was over I felt as though I could bounce that soccer ball off my head and it would sail across the whole city. I decided to walk the long way home, across the park. Gardeners were digging up the flower beds and I breathed in that damp dirt smell. It seemed to fill up my whole head. Maybe an hour of heading had dislodged my brain, leaving an empty space filled with a kind of quiet buzz.

Head banging. Maybe that was why Emma thumped her head against the wall . . . My heart fell to my stomach. Emma. Was this Thursday? Oh, don't let it be Thursday. It was Thursday. I'd promised Mom I'd be home at five to take care of Emma till Dad got home. And it was already—I ripped open the velcro cuff on my jacket—five-thirty. I ran the rest of the way home and when I got to the corner I saw Grandpa getting out of a taxi and Mom exploding out the front door holding Emma.

"I'm sorry. I forgot. We had a long practice."

Mom dumped Emma in Grandpa's arms. "Rachel. The one day I ask you to be here to take care of her. Now I'm going to be late for work. What would I have done if Grandpa hadn't been able to come?"

"It's okay," said Grandpa. "I don't mind coming over."

Mom got in the car, slammed the door, and took off.

"She has always *hated* being late," said Grandpa, "even when she was really little. I wouldn't worry about it too much."

"Are you going to go home again?"

"I don't think so. I figure if I stick around here somebody will give me dinner. Dinner with two charming ladies." He jiggled Emma in his arms and she smiled.

I knew that if Grandpa continued being nice I was going to lose it and cry so I excused myself with homework and went to my room.

The faint buzz in my head had turned into a hive of angry bees. So I made a mistake. I'm *sorry*. But who asked my opinion about Emma coming here, anyway? I just don't like her. You're allowed not to like somebody. I don't appreciate being woken up every night for one thing. I know you think she's really cute. And so do Dad and Daniel and, like, the whole rest of the universe, but I don't. She just creeps me out. Okay?

I went to the bathroom to get Kleenex and on the way back I glanced into the living room. Grandpa was singing and dancing with Emma standing on his feet. He used to do that with me. I went in my room and put on my headphones.

When Dad told me that Emma was going home the next Monday I was relieved. I was looking forward to life without her.

Until last Sunday night, that is.

It was just after dinner. Mom was out. Dad and Daniel and I were goofing around in the kitchen, sort of cleaning up, but really spreading chocolate sauce on saltine crackers as a post-dessert dessert. Emma was sitting on the kitchen stool eating crackers and not dripping.

Daniel was going on an ecology field trip the next day and Dad was giving him a hard time. "Sounds like a holiday to me. A taxpayer-subsidized in-term holiday. Wouldn't have happened in my day. Nose to the grindstone we were, steeped in the work ethic."

Daniel rolled his eyes at me. "Dad, you're such a fraud. I happen to know, from an inside source, that you spent your whole grade-twelve year spaced out on the Mothers of Invention, writing poetry about, like, dead squirrels, and doing absolutely no work at all."

Dad threw his tea towel in the air and roared. "Inside source! It's Uncle Wally, isn't it? The fink! I'll kill him. But first—you."

Dad played rugby in high school and sometimes it still comes over him. He tackled Daniel and threw him to the kitchen floor. They rolled over a few times and I turned away. An audience only encourages them.

And then I saw Emma. She was a dead fish-belly white. And before I could say anything, or go to her, she jumped down off the stool and threw herself onto Dad's back, beating him with her fists. Dad tried to reach around behind him and by doing so crushed Daniel, who couldn't get out. I ran over and unglued Emma from Dad's back. She began to hit me but I held her tight in my arms. I sat on the floor. "Emma. It's okay. It's just pretend. Dad's just playing. It's okay."

I don't think she could hear me. She was shaking her head and whispering "no" on each shake. Her eyes were shut tight. I just held on. Dad and Daniel found their own legs and arms and scooted across the floor to us. We all sat in a tight little knot, me holding Emma, Dad and Daniel holding me.

The *no*'s turned to sobs. Tears leaked out from under her eyelids. And then, in the space of one deep, ragged breath, the little tight doll-plastic body softened. I pushed the sweat-soaked red curls off her forehead and gently moved her pencil-point elbow from my stomach. She shifted in my arms, melting into me, and then, with her eyes still closed, she reached up and grabbed my earlobe, holding on. There was silence in the kitchen and into that silence slimed a piece of knowing that had not been there before.

That night after Emma was asleep, Dad called the family-care worker. She arrived about the same time Mom got home and they all sat in the living room and talked for a long time. I went down and watched junk videos with Daniel in the basement. Later Dad called us upstairs and told us that Emma was still going home the next afternoon.

"No way," said Daniel.

I remembered how I had wished her gone and tried to vacuum back those wishes. Dad ran his fingers through his hair. "They know much more about the situation than we do, Daniel."

Daniel kicked the wall. "What, are you blind? You were there. Somebody in that family gets hit. What if it's her?"

"They *are* her parents, Daniel. And they've had help," said Mom. "Family Services is confident that it's the best thing for her under the circumstances."

"Yeah. Right."

From the room along the hall came the familiar soft thumping. Daniel stood up, screeching his chair along the floor, and crashed down the basement stairs to his room. Dad and Mom and I went in to hold on to Emma.

Daniel was gone by the time I woke up the next day. I said I had a headache and then Mom, who sometimes gets her lines just right, said why didn't I stay home from school because there is no point trying to learn when you're not well.

"Why don't you go in and check on Emma? I've told her that she's going home today. But I can't tell how she's taking it."

When I went into Emma's room she was sitting in front of the dollhouse, clutching something in her fist.

"What do you have?"

She held out her hand and opened it. There was a little plastic action figure, a man dressed in skintight green. He had grotesque lumpy muscles. Clear proof of steroid use if you ask me. He had one eye in the middle of his forehead.

Max heaved himself up off the floor and padded over. He sniffed the figure and gave a quiet "ah-roo."

"Who's this?" I asked.

"It's the Guy," said Emma. "Look." She held him up and pushed his stomach and the red eye lit up.

"Cool. Does he live here?"

"Yes," said Emma, and she put the Guy into bed between Mother and Father and covered them with one of her socks.

I could just hear Daniel. "Suburban sex scandal. Housewife tells all." He must have left the figure as a good-bye present for Emma. Sometimes he's so completely weird.

We ate animal crackers instead of breakfast and didn't bother getting dressed. Mom brought the ironing board into Emma's room and ironed her wardrobe while we played. A hot clean smell filled the room. The Guy got out of bed and started to heal things. One blast from his uni-eye cured my sore toe and my sore knee and my sore belly button and my sore eyelashes. "All fixed, all fixed, bibbedy, bobbedy, boo," said Emma. Then he fixed Mom. We ran out of body parts before Emma ran out of interest. So we turned to the Nuclear family.

Amazingly, all the Nuclears seemed to have the same ailments as me. The red light blinked and Emma's voice became a chant as she spoke for the Guy.

"Sore toe, all fixed. Sore knee, all fixed. Sore belly button, all fixed. Bibbedy, bobbedy, boo."

I launched out a bit and idly picked up Mother, last in line for the miracle cure. I picked her up by her purple arm.

Emma has that very white skin that redheads sometimes have. So white it is almost transparent, easily bruised. I reached over and pulled her into my lap, wrapping my arms around her. I rested my chin on her soft curls for just a second. Now was just fine. Why couldn't she just stay here? Then she wriggled in my arms like a lizard and escaped. Her voice was very indignant. "Rachel! I'm playing."

We packed Emma's things very neatly into her suitcases. But she wouldn't let us pack the Guy. She wouldn't let go of him, even when she ate lunch. He gave his glowing healing touch to her milk, her crackers, and to all the noodles in her soup.

We read *Cinderella* one last time. I had it memorized. I said the words and wondered about the fairy godmother, and how she knew just when to turn up, and how brave it was of Cinderella to go to the ball in the first place. I thought about "happily ever after" and "the best situation under the circumstances."

The family-care worker came after lunch. I didn't cry until her car was leaving. But as it pulled into the traffic I saw Emma through a blur of tears. She was holding the Guy up to the window. He flashed a red good-bye.

A few days later Daniel and I packed up the dollhouse. Some of the metal tabs snapped off as Daniel bent them back with pliers.

I wrapped the Nuclears in paper. "Never mind," I told them

silently. "It won't be long. The Russians are coming." I had seen a brochure on the kitchen table. It was about this program for bringing Russian children to Canadian families for the summer, children from radiation-contaminated areas, to give them good food and clean air and medicine. I figured we would be getting one.

"Oh, rats, there goes another one. I think this house is toast."

"No, it's not. Somebody could fix it with solder or something."

"Yeah, maybe." Daniel pulled off the roof and slid it into the storage box. Max padded into the room.

Daniel addressed some spot over my head. "I think we should find her and steal her back."

"That's a totally excellent idea."

"We could wear stocking masks and drive an unmarked van and . . ." Daniel looked at me.

I tried. "Tot rescued in daring heist. Teenage kidnappers vow . . . teenage kidnappers vow . . ." But it didn't work. We were both playing with someone who wasn't really playing.

Max stuck his nose into the roofless house.

"Hey, Dan. The Guy was a big hit. Did Mom tell you?"

"What guy?"

"That little green action figure you left for Emma. Mr. Testosterone. She loved him."

"I didn't leave her anything."

"Come on. Honest?"

"Honest."

"Then where did it come from?"

"Search me." There was a screech of metal as Daniel pulled off the back of the house. Max fled.

I wrapped up Baby. Smiling, unchanging Baby Nuclear. Happy all the time. I nestled him down into the box.

The Guy. I don't know. A visitor who came when he was needed? I just hope, wherever she's gone to, that Emma's holding on to him tight.

All fixed now, all fixed, all fixed, bibbedy, bobbedy, boo.

V I S I T O R S

We started up the rocky streambed trail. The stones shifted under my boots. My right big toe was not happy and my pack already felt heavy. A coalition of my legs and stomach decided to report to me that this hike was a dumb idea. Ahead of me Ellen was setting an ambitious pace.

"Hey, Ellen, slow down a bit. And just remind me. I forgot for a minute. Why is it fun to haul your body up the side of a mountain?"

One thing about old friends. You can count on them to be sensitive and sympathetic when you are needy or troubled.

"Come on, droop-head, you're always like this for the first twenty minutes. Don't forget. No pain, no gain."

I trudged along, wondering when I could suggest a mountain mix break. Then I fantasized about how much I would like to hike the Grand Canyon, where you get to go down first. And then I thought for about the eleventh time how amazing it was that Ellen and I were here at all.

In our minds it was the "weekend hike to the cross-country ski hut." In our parents' minds it was mission intergalactica or something. They thought of many dire fates that awaited us. Ellen and I have seven parents between us. That's a lot of interparental phone calls. But finally we persuaded them. My wild card was that I reminded my mother that she was only one year older than me when she went off to Europe on her own. It is a good idea to pay attention when parents are discussing their youths. It can often make useful ammunition. Really, though, I think they let us go because my parents think Ellen is very responsible and Ellen's parents, well, they let Ellen do pretty much what she wants. They're a bit scared of her ever since she was in the hospital.

Ellen was still setting a "we have to be at K^2 before nightfall so don't spare the Sherpas" kind of pace.

"Hey, Ellen, if each of our parents phoned each of our other parents, how many calls would that be?

Ellen paused. "The formula would be number of parents minus one plus number of parents minus two and so on. In our case it would be, let's see, six plus five plus four plus three plus two plus one equals twenty-one."

Ellen's mathematical pause gave me a chance to catch up and get out my mountain mix before she could set off again.

The trail got steeper. Ellen led and I caught up. This is more or less how our friendship has been since we met in Tiny Tutus for Two's. According to Dad, Ellen grabbed my hand the first day of ballet and showed me exactly what to do. I don't remember this. I don't remember a time when I didn't know Ellen.

After about half an hour my body parts stopped whining and the trail widened out. Sun splashed through the trees and the only sound was the scuff of our boots. I tried to cover everything with snow to turn it into the familiar ski trail. But this was a new world, of dark and pale green and the soft warm smell of forest dirt.

After lunch we got a case of the early afternoon stupidos, and we started talking without our tongues. This is a method of talking that Ellen invented in grade four. The idea is that you leave your tongue limp on the bottom of your mouth and try to talk. Ellen recited the "tomorrow and tomorrow and tomorrow" speech from *Macbeth*. Then I sang "On Top of Spaghetti." Then we both fell on the ground.

There are probably some people who think we should have outgrown dead-tongue talk by now. But it can really be a riot. Go on, try it. Rest your tongue on the bottom of your mouth and sing, "With glowing hearts . . ." No? Well, maybe you had to be there.

My favorite moment hiking is when you come up above the tree line. Everything opens up and becomes light outside and inside, and you feel like the discoverer of the top of the world. It was about five o'clock when we left the forest behind us. The air was suddenly crisper and I gulped it in. "I feel like I'm breathing helium."

"If you were breathing helium, you would sound like Donald Duck," said Ellen, who knows many odd facts. "We should be at the hut in about an hour."

My legs were just starting to ask questions again when we arrived. The hut looked different in the summer, naked without its cover of snow. But inside there were ghosts of winter, the faint smells of wet woolen socks and soup-in-a-mug.

I was all for an immediate supper, but Ellen wanted to unpack first. As she laid out the contents of her pack on one of the wooden benches along the wall, I was treated to a vision of minimal packing at its most intense. We had discussed traveling light and I felt I had made the ultimate sacrifice by bringing only two books. But Ellen had brought an individual portion of toothpaste, screwed up in a piece of waxed paper, and a single length of dental floss.

I left her in her organizational mode and went around to the back of the cabin. There was a clearing, a big flat piece of rock covered in moss and lichen. The orange warning flashers that the ski patrol puts up in winter to keep people from skiing off the edge were gone. I went to the edge and sat with my feet over. I tossed a small stone and it went tumbling down the rocky slope, bouncing and ricocheting. I looked out over the deep green valley. And then I flopped onto my back. The moss was soft and the warmth of the sun-heated rock radiated through the thin covering and onto my arms and the back of my knees. I turned my head and looked through one eye at the moss world. A dozen shades of green and brown and little stems with flowers. I made myself the size of a ladybug and went on a hike through the moss world. Pale green lichen like frost flowers. I closed both eyes and the world tipped slightly. I took off my boots, stripped off my sweaty socks, and wiggled my toes in the helium air.

For supper we had sandwiches. I ate three plus a chocolate bar and a peach yogurt. Ellen ate a few bites of yogurt and the filling out of one sandwich. She fed the bread to a whiskey jack. Three more birds appeared, looking with greedy and unafraid eyes at our provisions. I kept a protective hand over the granola bars.

After supper we sat on the bench at the back of the hut and played insult alphabet. Ellen had just called me a quisling and I was about to call her a reprobate when they came around the corner of the house.

I didn't see them clearly at first because I was looking right into the setting sun. A moviemaker couldn't have done it better, the sun lighting them from behind, their red-blond hair glowing like halos. They were tall. They looked remarkably alike. And they were beautiful. Cheekbones, symmetry, sea-green eyes, hair like polished silk. We're not talking cute here. We're talking stare and be stunned.

"Hello," said one, the male one. "Can we visit?"

They didn't look like the drug-crazed ax murderers that our seven parents had warned us about so I said, "Sure." Ellen didn't answer.

They walked across the clearing and sat down on the ground next to us. They didn't seem to sit down so much as to float to ground level. Their clothes, layers of pale light cotton, settled around them. I wondered if they were dancers.

Afterward Ellen and I couldn't remember what we talked about with them. We tried to piece together what we knew about them and it wasn't much. Their names were Sith and Bab. They were brother and sister. Not twins although they sure looked it. They were camping somewhere "over there"—one waved toward Salmonberry Flats. They didn't go to school.

There was only one bit of conversation I remember clearly. Sith slid down onto one elbow and said, "I have a white case, an inner case of velvet, and gold at the heart."

I tried to catch Ellen's eye. Was this guy on something or what?

But she was staring at him with that look she sometimes gets in math class.

Concentration, admiration, and challenge. "An egg," she replied.

Again I tried to roll my eyes at Ellen. How corny. We hadn't played riddles since about grade three. I stretched back to find one. What's green and plays the guitar?

Ellen beat me to it. "I have a fat little body, six arms, no legs. I can cover the mountains and fill the valleys and some day I could become a man."

I was just as glad she had beaten me to the draw. Elvis Pickle was seriously outclassed in this company. I elbowed my way in. "It's a spider, right? Like, it could become a man. Spider-Man. And covering the mountains. Like that could be a whole bunch of spiders. Is that it?"

Bab and Sith looked at each other and at Ellen. There was an invisible cobweb joining them, a sparkling electrical current that definitely didn't include me. They weren't even listening to me. I wanted the visitors to go away.

Then Bab and Sith each gave a little explosive sigh at the same time, as though they had been holding their breaths. These guys obviously took their riddles seriously.

"A snowflake," said Bab.

Sith gave a little smile, but only with his mouth. "It is higher than the highest thing, lower than the lowest thing, better than God, worse than the devil. The dead eat it but if you eat it you die."

Ellen was thinking so hard that I could almost see her head glow. Finally she seemed to slump. I wondered if I could lighten things up with my Alexander the Grape riddle. Probably not.

"I give up," she said.

"You'll know later," said Sith.

The sun went down and Ellen and I put on sweatshirts, but the visitors didn't seem to feel the cold. And then, just at the moment when I wanted to go in and light the stove in the hut, Sith took out a mouth organ. He started out with that sucking sound that mouth-organ players seem to warm up with. I always think it sounds like a train in the distance. When he started to play, it went right into my feet, bypassing my brain entirely. I slipped my boots back on. Bab grabbed the spoons from our empty yogurt containers and licked them, the way people lick the last of their ice-cream cones. Then she began to tap them together, running them over the fingers of one hand and against her thigh.

Before I had decided to, I was on my feet dancing around that rocky place like a crazy person. Ellen, too. We couldn't stop. And I wasn't tired at all. My legs were like springs. I just wanted to dance harder and faster and longer and never to stop. Sweat broke out on my scalp. We danced the sun down and then, still dancing, I went into the hut and got a couple of candles and the matches. I moved a piece of kindling into the middle of the rocky clearing and drip-attached two candles to the wood. The night was so still that only the wind of our dancing made them flicker.

There was no moon, and the green valley turned into a dark pit. The whole world was there in that circle of candlelight. The visitors danced with us. Sith pulled his shirt out of his pants and it billowed out as he whirled. Bab's skirt stood out like a bell. We danced in ones and twos and threes and all together. The candle shadows sharpened their faces. Their eyes disappeared into deep shaded sockets.

Sweat ran down into my eyes and drops flew off the visitors through the light into the darkness. I was doing a step of my own invention, a sort of clogging hip-hop fusion, when I put my foot down hard onto the edge of a loose rock and pain flashed across my ankle. I tried to keep dancing but each step was worse. So I hopped over to the bench and collapsed onto it. Nobody seemed to notice. I considered feeling left out and sorry for myself but I couldn't do it. Not with that music swirling around the candlelit circle, around my brain. My pounding heart calmed down and I lifted my hair off my neck and held it on top of my head.

I wondered if I had broken my ankle. I thought about having to be rescued by a helicopter. Whappity, whappity, whappity.

Then Sith yelled something, one word, and the music seemed to flip into a higher gear of speed and volume. He sure could get an amazing sound from that little mouth organ.

Ellen and Bab were holding hands and whirling in a tight little circle around Sith. Then Ellen let go for a moment and slid off her flannel shirt, hurling it out of the circle. Underneath she was wearing a dark tank top, and when I squinted at her I could merge the top and the surrounding darkness so that Ellen looked like a head and arms with no body. Then she danced close to the light and I got a flash glimpse at her upper arms and I felt cold. They were like dowels. She was still so skinny.

Three years ago Ellen stopped eating. She nearly died. And I nearly stopped being her friend. I nearly stopped because I started to be too careful.

Have you ever noticed how often you mention food in the course of an ordinary conversation—"What's for dinner?" "I'm starving." People don't with Ellen. Like when we were planning this trip. Bryce said (Bryce is my father number two), "What are you planning to do about food?" And when he asked there was a little pause, a little hairline crack between "about" and "food." A little icy hairline crack.

After Ellen got out of the hospital, she started eating again. Well, sort of. But because she nearly died I was scared of her. So I was really careful, too. But those little hairline cracks widened and soon she was on the other side of the Grand Canyon. Our friendship was saved by fajitas.

We had been out to a movie. It was a weeper. We used a pack of Kleenex each.

Tragedy always gives me an appetite and it felt so much like before—both of us crying in a movie—that I suggested we drop into, tentative little pause, the Sunshine Cafe.

Ellen gave a little wince but said okay.

Ellen wouldn't look at the menu so I ordered fajitas for both of us. They were fabulous, full of sautéed peppers, red and yellow, big sweet pieces of fried onion, all smothered in melted cheese and sour cream. I finished mine off in about four transcendent bites. But Ellen just kept pushing hers around the plate.

And suddenly I had had it. I wanted that fajita. I was furious with Ellen. Furious with her for nearly dying and for wasting her fajita.

"If you're going to treat that thing like a dead rat, give it to me."

First of all Ellen tried that "how cruel of you to say such a thing to me" look, but she couldn't keep it up. Her mouth started trembling and then she was laughing and snorting and crying again. She had to blow her nose on her napkin. "Dead rat," she kept repeating.

She impaled the fajita with her fork and sailed it across the table to my plate. Then she looked deep into my eyes and said, "If I had only one dead rat, I would give it to you."

Since then I haven't been careful with Ellen.

But seeing her sticklike arms did make me feel a bit cold in my stomach. What had she actually eaten today? Almost nothing. Nothing.

Hey! "Nothing!" I yelled it out. "Nothing."

The dancers didn't hear me. I pivoted off the bench and hopped over. Ouch.

"Nothing," I bellowed.

Still they carried on. What, were they deaf or something? I ducked under their dancing arms and blew out the candles. The music stopped.

"The answer to the riddle is nothing."

"Katie." Ellen's voice was furious. "What did you do that for? What's with you?"

It's a lot darker out on the mountain at night than it is in the city. I heard confused movement and then Ellen said, "I'm going to get the flashlight."

I stood on one leg in the dark quiet and then the flashlight beam cut across the darkness. It scanned the whole circle.

"Bab? Sith?" Ellen yelled, and her voice echoed across the valley.

"They've gone," I said.

She shone the light into my eyes. "Thanks a lot."

"Well, it's not my fault if they take off just because I guess their dumb riddle."

I expected Ellen to argue with me, to tear a strip off me, but instead her voice got small. "Why did they have to go so soon?" She shone the flashlight out over the valley, where its thin beam was eaten up by darkness.

We crawled into our sleeping bags without speaking, without taking off our clothes.

Our silence filled the room like roaring. I tried to think of the one right thing to say, but in the middle of thinking I fell into sleep, abruptly, like falling off the edge of a cliff.

The next morning Ellen shook me awake. The minute my eyes opened I felt like a scumbag. "Are you mad? I'm sorry. I was really feeling left out and . . ."

But Ellen reached over and put her finger on my lips. "Shh. I've got something to show you. Come on."

I slid out of my sleeping bag and followed her out the door and around to the back of the cabin. The ground was cold on my bare feet and my ankle was a bit stiff but it seemed to work.

A light mist was moving across the clearing as dew steamed off the moss and rock.

And then I saw it. A circle. A circle where dancing feet had worn away the moss. A circle whose outer edge was a handsbreadth away from the crumbling cliff edge. I swallowed. There was something in my throat. "Who were they?"

Ellen shook her head. Then her face fell apart. Ellen, who doesn't cry except at movies. She pushed the words out between sobs. "I got up early. And I hiked over to Salmonberry Flats. There's nobody camping there. So I came back. I was just going to sit here. So I could see them again. Like they were last night. Perfect. I wanted them to be here. And then I noticed."

Ellen's arms were rigid at her sides, her hands clenched. I stepped up close behind her and rested my head on her shoulder. A whiskey jack bounced out of a tree, did a fly-by through the clearing looking for breakfast, and then, with a complaining cry, flew out over the deep green valley.